FRAMED IN CORNWALL

JANIE BOLITHO

Allison & Busby Limited
12 Fitzroy Mews
London W1T 6DW
allisonandbusby.com

First published in Great Britain in 1998.
This paperback edition published by Allison & Busby in 2015.

A CIP catalogue record for this book is available from
the British Library.

10 9 8 7 6 5 4 3 2

ISBN 978-0-7490-1779-8

Typeset in 10.5/15.5 pt Sabon by
Allison & Busby Ltd.

The paper used for this Allison & Busby publication
has been produced from trees that have been legally sourced
from well-managed and credibly certified forests.

Printed and bound by
CPI Group (UK) Ltd, Croydon, CR0 4YY

JANIE BOLITHO was born in Falmouth, Cornwall. She enjoyed a variety of careers – psychiatric nurse, debt collector, working for a tour operator, a book-maker's clerk – before becoming a full-time writer. She passed away in 2002.

For my aunt, Con Gardner

CHAPTER ONE

Dorothy Pengelly sniffed the top of the carton of milk and shrugged. The expiry date had elapsed but it smelt all right and the cats wouldn't notice. One of her uncles used to drink a pint of sour milk every day of his adult life and he had lived to be over ninety. Dorothy did not use milk in her tea or put butter on her bread, she could not abide dairy products.

She had three cats and two dogs, one of them a retired racing Greyhound an old friend up Exeter way had given her, the other a snarling Jack Russell.

Her granite-built house was none too clean but only because she refused to admit that her eyesight was not as good as it once was so she was unable to spot the cobwebs or the spills on the flagstone floor. The place was too large for her but she would never move. It had been her home all her married life and she intended dying in it. Besides, she knew the number of years left to her were limited and she could not bear the idea of upheaval.

She filled the three saucers which were lined up in front of the metal legs of the ancient cooker. They had concentric circles of cream in them ending in yellow crusts. Peter; she smiled wryly. Her son couldn't wait for her to die. He and Gwen would sell their house in Hayle and move into something far too grand for them. Her son had married unwisely. Gwen was a schemer and tended to forget that Peter had a brother. Martin might not be as bright as Peter but he was her flesh and blood and she loved him dearly. Oh, well, she thought, they would all find out in time.

Her will, made on a visit to Truro with Martin, would give several people a shock. Her assets were worth a lot more than many imagined and Rose Trevelyan had put her wise as to the value of her paintings.

The house was situated on sloping ground between outcrops of boulders. The grass between them was tough, seasoned by the blistering sun and the harsh winter storms which swept mercilessly over the terrain. One or two stunted trees, bent to the angle of the winds, barely survived but the low gorse thrived and flowered twice a year when its almond scent filled her nostrils and made her nostalgic for her youth. In the distance was the glimmer of the sea although, on dull days, it merged greyly with the sky on the horizon.

There were two outhouses, one of which was almost in ruins. The other was only suitable for storing junk as the corrugated iron roof leaked. At one time the dogs had slept there until Dorothy had finally relented and allowed them into the house. The cats were never to be seen at night.

Once a week she got a lift into Camborne or Penzance with Jobber Hicks, a neighbouring farmer she had known since childhood, and whom she had once seriously considered marrying. Apart from those shopping expeditions she rarely went out. Fred Meecham used to share a pot of tea with her when he dropped off her groceries, but not so frequently now that Marigold was so ill. In fact, although he had called in two days ago she hardly saw him at all and she had an uncomfortable feeling she knew the reason why. But there was a lot for Fred to come to terms with, she did not know how he would cope when Marigold finally went. Rose's visits were awaited with pleasure. If the weather was fine, they would take a stroll or go out in the car and have tea in a cafe. Dorothy decided to give Rose a ring and ask if she would mind bringing over a couple of pints of milk when she came tomorrow.

Rose stood in her lounge window in the manner of someone waiting for a guest. In her hand was a mug of coffee. She stared across the wide expanse of Mount's Bay trying to make up her mind what the weather was going to do.

The view was spectacular and ever-changing. On clear days she could see the white sands of the beaches of Marazion and the whole of St Michael's Mount rising majestically, almost menacingly, out of the sea. To her left was Newlyn harbour where beam trawlers and netters came and went without pattern. On some days a jumble of masts could be seen, on others there were few. It was landing day. The tuna season was over but she had returned from the fish market with two large monk tails which had cost her next to nothing because she knew most of the fishermen.

In the kitchen she rinsed out her mug and inverted it on the draining-board. Through the window which looked out over the sloping garden she could see more and more patches of blue appearing between the clouds but, knowing the inconsistencies of the weather in West Cornwall, she decided to take a waterproof jacket anyway.

Leaving the house by the side entrance which led directly into the kitchen, Rose got into her Mini which was parked on the steep narrow drive beside the house. It started first time because it had recently been serviced. Trevor, the husband of her best friend, Laura, fished out of Newlyn. He had his engineer's ticket and could make sense of any machinery. Rose's car was child's play to him. As he refused payment Rose had bought him a bottle of Jack Daniel's and a packet of his favourite tobacco. Despite the service Rose knew it was time for the Mini to go. For a painter a vehicle was not indispensable, but in her other role as a photographer it was essential. Her equipment with its heavy lenses was impossible to lug around on foot or by public transport.

She backed down the precarious drive with the ease of years of practice, negotiated the bend at the bottom and waited for the Mousehole bus, along with a stream of cars held up behind it, to pass. When it was safe to do so she pulled out and drove down into Newlyn village and turned left for Lamorna Cove.

She was fully aware of her hesitation in changing the car. David had bought it for her. But David was dead and although he had died five years ago it would seem like a betrayal of sorts. He would have wanted you to be practical not sentimental, she told herself, recalling how very different they had been – yet the marriage had worked, had been happier than most.

Rose planned to make some sketches of the cove. She had

been commissioned to do a series of watercolours of some of the small Cornish bays. Once complete they would be reproduced on the front of notelets which would be packaged along with envelopes, ten to a box. She had decided to depict each from a high vantage point so that she could include the granite cottages which sloped down to the bays. It did not matter at this stage if it rained for Rose would only be concentrating on the outline and scale.

The car park on the quay was busy. Lamorna, with its one hotel and its one pub, the Lamorna Wink, was always popular with holidaymakers and walkers. There were still plenty of people around although the children had gone back to school. In the gently moving water protected by the harbour wall were several divers. Sitting on the wall, legs swinging into the void, were others, their wetsuits gleaming.

Rose turned and began walking. In the distance three people could be seen making their way up the steep cliff path which led back to Newlyn. Glancing at her watch she saw that she had two hours before she was due in Penzance. She slung her canvas bag over one shoulder and began the ascent which would make her calves ache but would lead her to a sheltered vantage point. Her hair, the lighter strands mingling with the auburn, was tied back against the breeze which became stronger the higher she climbed. Twice she stopped to allow walkers to pass in single file.

Between two boulders covered with rough green and yellow lichen, Rose laid down a waterproof sheet and removed an A5 sketchpad and pencils from her bag. She wriggled into a comfortable position, resting her back against a smooth patch of the cliff. The drawings would be smaller than the paper size so she made the necessary allowance. Dressed in old jeans which were faded and threadbare at the knees and a thick checked shirt which had been David's, she was warm enough in the lee of the rocks towering above her.

The patches of blue had all but disappeared and within half an hour the sky was a uniform grey but the rain held off. Herring-gulls glided overhead and occasionally swooped, squawking noisily when they spotted people in the car park who were foolish enough to produce food. The birds had become a nuisance in recent years and signs had been put up in many resorts entreating visitors not to feed them, but Rose liked their arrogance and aggression although she was doubtful if they knew any longer what a herring was. Their staple diet consisted of chips, pasties and burgers. She would include their graceful flight in the sketch; two of them, she decided, their lateral feathers spread as they soared effortlessly.

An hour and a quarter later her back ached. Getting to her feet she stretched then picked up the sketchpad to study it. Satisfied with what she had produced she packed up. In no particular hurry she stayed for a while, relaxing under the changing sky. Lying on the waterproof she linked her hands behind her head and gazed into nothingness, emptying her mind. It was something she rarely had a chance to do. By the time she left the sea had changed from grey to green with a silken sheen where a ray of sunlight was reflected off the surface. A warm stillness had settled over the cove.

She knew she had been in danger of falling asleep. Many of her nights were restless since she no longer had the security of David's body beside her. It was not fear of living alone as much as simply knowing he wasn't there. They had not had any children but to Rose it was no longer a matter for regret. They had had each other.

Before she reached the car she went over the things she had planned for the next couple of days. This afternoon she had arranged to see Barry Rowe and later she was to photograph a Mrs Morgan's daughter whose eighteenth birthday it was. Informal shots would no doubt be taken at whichever night club the girl ended up in but her mother wanted one which she could frame. Tomorrow was Friday and she would be seeing Dorothy Pengelly. Rose smiled. What a character that lady is, she thought. And tonight, Jack Pearce. The smile faded. She had been seeing him on and off for more than a year. The relationship had not followed the usual form of progression and Rose was not sure of her feelings, only that they were ambiguous. They met when it was mutually convenient and enjoyed each other's company when they did so. But Jack, she knew, wanted more from her than she was able to give. Alone for so long, Rose had grown used to her independence and, in a way, so had Jack, whose hours were erratic, but she suspected he was one of those men who would prefer to live with a woman than without one.

Heading back along the country roads she was glad of the easy familiarity she felt with Barry Rowe. He was an old friend and the only person she allowed to call her Rosie, because he had given her her first break when she came to Cornwall all those years ago and because he had always been in love with her. What she had offered was friendship, no more than that, but she was vain enough to be flattered by his attentions.

* * *

Detective Inspector Jack Pearce had had a busy summer. From the moment the season proper had started crime had escalated. Not that he kidded himself that this branch of the Devon and Cornwall police had quite as much to contend with as the city boys who were stationed in Plymouth or Exeter. And he should know. He had spent several years in the force in Leeds. Of course the warm weather brought an influx of visitors and more people meant more crime. It also brought a lot of dropouts to the area. This was not to say that the locals could not make just as much of a nuisance of themselves but the police generally knew where to find them. Recently he had been involved in one of the biggest drug hauls in the West Country.

Tapping a pen against his teeth he wondered what Rose was doing at that moment and if she was thinking of him. He smiled his wolfish smile. That was extremely doubtful. She had probably taken herself to some isolated spot and was immersed in the scenery. Even on a day like today she could find beauty in something. Was she viewing it with her artist's eye or through the lens of a camera? Jack found it hard to believe she was only two years his junior, she was so petite and youthful. He towered over her by eight inches. He was solidly built with the typical dark Cornish colouring. Although his accent had been diluted by the years he had spent away from the area it was still strong enough to identify his origins.

Petty crime annoyed him. The perpetrators were rarely caught and the victims suffered out of all proportion to what the criminals gained. He sighed. He couldn't wait to see Rose that evening and wished he could see her more often. But at least he knew where he stood with her. Rose had made it quite clear that she would not give up her friends to spend more time with him. He accepted there was no choice but to make the best of what little he had. It was, he realised, little enough.

It had finally happened, the dreaded time when Marigold needed to be hospitalised. For months Fred had coped, running the shop but relying more and more on his staff, keeping the flat clean and seeing to Marigold's needs. As she weakened he had received outside help. Cheerful nurses were in and out of the upstairs flat several times a day.

Tears ran down his face as he thought of Marigold in that high bed, intravenous fluids running into her wasted arm. It had been so hard to leave her there. Barely able to speak she had managed a few whispered words. 'No one could've done so much for me. I love you, Fred.' It was the first time she had said it and he would remember it for ever. All he had done had been worth it in the end. Yes, he decided, even . . . but he would not allow himself to complete the thought.

He stared at his surroundings. The flat was cold and empty without Marigold. Kneeling, he tried to pray but no words came. Not since his boyhood had he missed church on Sunday but he thought he would stop going now. Sometimes he found it hard to believe he worshipped the same God as the rest of the congregation. The one he knew was a personal friend with whom he held conversations. How could He have time for all those others, for the women, some of whom still wore hats and who gossiped outside after the service? His parents had been strict Methodists, bringing him up to fear shame and dishonesty, to act in a way which could not offend or cause gossip. He had not caused gossip, he had been very careful on that score.

Fred had offered his soul in return for Marigold's health. All he had ever desired was someone loyal and kind, someone worth loving, someone worth living for. Whilst many paid lip service to the familiar words of the litany Fred silently communed with God. He had suffered and he had paid the price of his sins. She would not pay the price of hers, he had seen to that, but without her he was nothing.

Dorothy Pengelly's younger son, Martin, had just passed his thirty-fourth birthday but looked much younger. He knew what people said about him, that he was simple, that he wasn't all there, and it hurt. Worse, it made him self-conscious and confused in strange company, which only served to perpetuate the myth. Alone he was a different man. Only his mother understood him fully and accepted him as he was. In return he loved her unconditionally.

Martin lived in a caravan which had been abandoned some years ago. Technically he was a squatter but it was unlikely anyone would return to claim it now. He had been out walking one day when he first discovered it about a mile from his mother's house. It was on rough ground, surrounded by clumps of bramble and obviously uninhabited. Many times he had returned but it remained empty and was becoming dilapidated. One day he had plucked up the courage to try the door. It was unlocked but the handle was stiff. On closer inspection he saw why it had been abandoned; it was fit only for the scrap heap. To Martin it was a challenge. He spent a month making repairs which may not have been aesthetic but which were effective. A few weeks later, when he was certain no one was going to lay claim to the van, he packed up his belongings and moved in, knowing that his mother would be pleased at this first step towards independence.

His income came solely from government benefits because despite his efforts to find work there was nothing at which he was able to succeed. The few employers who had given him a chance mistook his insecurity and shyness for stupidity and he had been asked to leave.

The caravan was comfortable and equipped with a battery-operated radio, Calor gas for cooking and heating, an oil lamp and a pile of pornographic magazines which he bought surreptitiously when he went to Truro. To Martin the women were not sexual objects but real people who would not laugh at him and snigger behind his back in the way in which the local girls did. His only downfall was drink. He couldn't handle it in the way other men seemed to. When he had money he walked into Hayle or Camborne and drank pints of cider and let his mouth run away with him. It allowed him to feel normal, part of a society from which he mostly felt excluded. When people spoke to him when he had drink inside him he was neither tongue-tied nor confused but he always suffered for it the next morning.

Once a month Peter, his brother, would invite him for Sunday lunch. No one particularly enjoyed these visits, least of all Gwen, Peter's wife, but none of them seemed capable of breaking with tradition. The invitations had originally been extended to please Dorothy because she had suggested it would be good for Martin and there was her inheritance to consider. Martin had not known how to refuse. He felt uncomfortable in the almost sterile atmosphere of Peter's house but his niece and nephew enjoyed the hour he spent with them, playing, before they ate.

He had woken yesterday unable to remember quite when Mrs Trevelyan was coming to see his mother; the days were all the same to him. But she hadn't turned up. It would have been nice to have a friend of his own but where would he find one?

By the evening the air was heavy and oppressive. Martin studied the horizon as dusk fell. Tomorrow it would rain and there would probably be thunder. He sensed it and it made him restless but he had no money for a drink. Dorothy would lend him some, she often did. It was never begrudgingly, never handed over with anything other than a simple 'of course'. He always paid her back. This was one of the reasons why he was her favourite, one which Peter, who was encouraged by Gwen to push for all he could get, could not understand.

Martin kicked at the springy turf with the heel of his shoe and stared in the direction of the house. Its squareness and the two tall chimneys were outlined blackly against the darkening sky. He walked towards it, his hands in his pockets. Pressing his forehead against the kitchen window he saw Dorothy sprawled in her high-backed chair over which a knitted patchwork blanket had been thrown to disguise the threadbare fabric. Voices from the radio reached him faintly but Dorothy was sound asleep, her mouth partly open, her knees apart and one of the cats curled into the cradle made by her skirt.

George, the Jack Russell, bristled then relaxed when he

saw it was Martin. The Greyhound did not stir. She was going deaf.

Martin had let himself in with his own key and helped himself to a ten-pound note from his mother's purse then left her a note in his rounded block capitals to say he had done so. 'I've lent ten pounds. Martin,' he wrote on the back of an envelope. There were six other banknotes of the same value in her purse so he knew he was not leaving her short. He kissed Dorothy gently on the forehead and made sure the lock on the back door clicked shut behind him.

Beads of sweat formed on his skin as he trudged across the scrubby slopes until he reached the main road into Camborne. There, in one of the pubs, he had spent all but a few pence of the ten pounds before he was bought a drink by a man whose name he could no longer recall. It was after midnight before he'd got back to the van and he'd fallen asleep, fully clothed, on top of his bunk. When he opened his eyes it was daylight and his head was thumping.

Barry Rowe's shop was in a prominent position in Penzance. He made his living producing greetings cards which sold throughout the country as well as locally. He also stocked maps and films and other bits and pieces that appealed to tourists. In the summer he kept the shop open until trade dropped off because the season was so short yet, surprisingly, he also made a reasonable income during the winter. Much of what was on display was based on the work of local artists or, at least, depicted local scenery. Rose Trevelyan provided him with two things: original watercolours, which he reproduced, and a sense of joy whenever he was in her

19

company. She also photographed landscapes which he sold on to postcard companies.

He had known her since she first arrived in Cornwall, having just completed three years at art college. She had come to study the Newlyn and St Ives artists for six months before taking up a career but she had never gone back. Oils had been her favourite medium and she'd initially sold one or two each year through the cafes and galleries which served as outlets, although photography had taken over now.

It had been love at first sight on Barry's part. He would never forget the day she bounced into the shop, her long flowing hair burnished copper by the sun which streamed through the open door. Her enthusiasm and vitality were almost tangible. Then she had been pretty; now, with maturity, she had become more than that.

Barry pushed his glasses up his nose. Every pair he had ever possessed worked loose and the habit, so strongly ingrained, caused him to do so when there was no need. He knew he was no great catch. His hair was greying and rather thin, his shoulders were stooped and he was underweight but his devotion to Rose had not ceased. He was long over the pain he had felt when David Trevelyan had walked into his shop to buy a birthday card. Rose had been there at the time and Barry bitterly regretted telling David that the artist was standing behind him. The look which Rose had given David had been identical to the one he had given her a few short months previously. With that simple introduction Barry had known that his chances were nil.

When David died Barry had been genuinely distressed because he had liked and admired the man and knew that he had made Rose happy. Shamefully he struggled to stifle the thought that Rose might now come to accept him as more than a friend. It had not happened. Then Jack Pearce arrived on the scene. At least Rose hadn't dropped him completely in favour of the arrogant Inspector Pearce.

At precisely one o'clock Rose walked through the door, surprising Barry who was used to her tardiness. He grinned. 'It's all yours,' he said to Heather who was the latest in a long line of temporary or part-time assistants.

'Oh, I expect I'll cope,' she said wryly, rather liking the serious man for whom she worked.

'We're going out?' Rose had only expected to collect payment for some work.

'Just up the road for a quickie. There's something I want to discuss with you so I thought you might as well buy me a pint.'

'Fair enough. As long as you're about to hand me an envelope containing a cheque.'

'Mercenary bitch.'

Rose laughed. 'It's taken you long enough to find that out.'

They strolled up to Causewayhead and entered the London Inn. The front bar was busy where a group of fishermen who had landed that morning, along with their women, had been making an early start. Rose acknowledged the ones she knew before following Barry around to the small back bar where he was already ordering their drinks. Rose handed over the money.

'Okay, I've kept to my side of the bargain.' She held out her hand.

Barry shook his head and reached into his jacket pocket, taking out the cheque which Rose had been expecting.

'Thanks,' she said, glancing quickly at the figure before stuffing it into her shoulder bag. It had taken her a long time to become businesslike about her transactions. Initially she had imagined a sponsor or agent would deal with the monetary side of things. Her financial position was now secure but without her work she would be lost. The house had been paid for upon David's death and the capital from his insurance policies paid the bills. What she earned gave her freedom. 'What was it you wanted to discuss?'

'How are you at wild flowers?'

'I can tell a daisy from a buttercup.'

'Honestly, Rose, you know what I mean.' He wished she would not grin at him in that way, it always made him want to kiss her. 'I'm talking about notelets, the usual, ten to the box and packaged nicely.'

'It's been done to death.'

'Yes but they're popular and I was thinking of a different angle.'

'Go on then.'

'This time with an appropriate background, something simple, say a cliff or a disused tin mine, something which shows where the plant can be found with the location printed on the bottom. Take a look at this.' He slid a sheet of paper across the table and pointed at it with a thin finger. 'See, like this. Western Gorse, common enough down here and in Wales, I believe, but rare elsewhere and there's—'

'All right, all right, I get the drift. You've obviously done your homework,' Rose interrupted before he could get too carried away, as he tended to with new projects. 'But isn't it a bit late in the year to be starting on something like this?'

'Aha, that's where you're right. I have done my homework. Most of the plants on the list flower until October. If you're not too tied up with other work you could make a start and finish the rest in the spring.'

Rose was impressed. Scrawled in Barry's untidy hand were the names and locations of over twenty wild flowers. She raised an eyebrow. 'Usual rate?'

'Of course.'

'Oh.' Rose chewed her lip thoughtfully. 'October? I might get wet feet.'

'Honestly, woman. Okay, plus five per cent.'

'It's a deal. Now I can't sit around all day drinking, I've got to go. Things to do, you know.'

Barry shook his head, grinning at her cheek. He rarely indulged in more than one or two pints, Rose enjoyed a drink far more than he did. The smile faded as she walked away and he was left to wonder if Jack Pearce was on her agenda.

Since the time Fred Meecham had taken over the shop in Hayle he had spent an hour or so with Dorothy Pengelly at least once a week. But that was before Marigold's illness had taken hold and he had discovered his secret might not be safe. Despite the difference in their ages they got on well. It had started when Dorothy had given up the car and begun sending in an order for heavy goods such as a case of cat or dog food which he delivered free of charge. A strange kind of friendship had developed. He knew she did not buy everything from him but he did not resent it. He understood

23

how much she enjoyed her trips to Camborne or even Truro with Jobber Hicks.

It was Dorothy to whom he had confessed that his wife had run off with a rep from a biscuit company who used to call at the shop. 'She took all she could carry,' he had told her, 'but she didn't take the boy.' Fred had been left to bring Justin up as best he could. Five years later, at the age of sixteen, Justin, too, had left home.

'Where did they go?' Dorothy had wanted to know.

'To hell as far as I care.' Fred had left it at that. He had tried hard to make the marriage work. Divorce was against his religious principles but Rita had gone away, waited the stipulated period and filed the papers without any resort to him.

He thought about what Dorothy had said a few years afterwards, when Marigold had moved in. 'Time you took over your own destiny, Fred. It's all very well your sister running your home and helping out in the shop but a man like you needs a wife.'

He had nodded and smiled and gone on to talk about the chrysanthemums he grew in the small garden behind the shop. Dorothy had made a joke about them being the wrong sort of flower, they ought to have been Marigolds.

She had been deeply sad when he came to say that Marigold had been diagnosed as having cancer. 'It's so unfair, she's so young.'

'I'd spend every penny I've got to find a cure,' Fred had continued. 'Every bloody penny. I want the best treatment money can buy.'

Dorothy had reassured him that she was probably getting

it anyway and that he would be wasting his time by paying for private care.

But Fred had not been able to let the matter go. 'I could send her to America. You read about people who get sent to specialists over there and get cured.'

How hopeful he had been in the early days of the disease. He had had an estate agent look over the shop and give him a valuation but even with his savings and any other money he could scrape together he knew he would never get Marigold to the States.

Was it too late? Wasn't there something he could do? Of course there was. He should not have allowed the pessimistic thoughts to arise.

Most days his staff would mind the shop whilst he paid a midday visit to Marigold in the hospital but he always spent a couple of hours with her again in the evenings. He pulled on his jacket. Tonight, once she became too tired to bear his company any longer, he would make his final attempt.

Fred Meecham locked the shop door knowing that things would turn out all right.

CHAPTER TWO

It had taken Martin most of Thursday to recover from his hangover. He spent the morning cleaning the caravan and washing out his socks and underpants. It was therapeutic, a way of cleansing himself, ridding his mind of the shame he felt at disgracing himself. They were chores which would have taken most people far less time but he always worked slowly and methodically, never undertaking more than one simple task at a time. He polished the windows inside and out, using newspaper soaked in vinegar as he had seen his mother do. As the morning wore on the chill of the past few days evaporated under a hot autumn sun. Martin removed the long seat cushions which doubled as mattresses at night and lugged them out to air, propping them against rocks.

In the afternoon he walked down to Hayle and cashed his unemployment cheque then bought a bagful of groceries, enough to last him the weekend. He got a cheap cut of meat, a loaf of bread and some fresh vegetables. It was after three when he had finished and he realised that he had enough money left over to repay his mother and just still be able to have a drink. Just one, he told himself. Hesitating only briefly he crossed the road, walked past the lane he should have taken to go home and went into the pub.

Glancing around he was relieved to see that there were only three other people present, none of whom he recognised. The two men he had spoken to on his previous visit must have gone back to wherever it was they came from. They had not been local but he could not place their accent. Martin had not set foot outside Cornwall and things which occurred on the other side of the Tamar Bridge were of no interest to him. He decided they had been holidaymakers and left it at that.

He jangled the coins in the pocket of his jeans and resisted the temptation to buy a second pint of cider. He felt worse rather than better for the one he had drunk.

The walk home helped to clear his head. Instinctively his feet picked their way through gorse roots and scattered stones. For a big man he moved lightly and easily and all the walking kept him fit. He stowed his groceries in cupboards in the caravan then walked down to the house.

'What's up, son?' Dorothy asked as soon as she saw his face. No answer was necessary, the way he was trembling and refusing to meet her eyes said it all.

'Nothing, Ma.'

'You've bin drinking again.' It was a statement. She wiped her hands on a tea towel and studied him carefully before turning to stir something simmering in a pot. 'You'll end up in trouble if you don't look out.' Martin was not dishonest, nor was he a fighting man, but he was easily taken advantage of, especially when he had drink inside him. How unalike her boys were. Peter was much the brighter but he lacked compassion.

Martin was insecure, easily hurt and quickly ashamed yet he intuitively offered comfort whenever it was needed.

Peter imagined that, because she insisted on his repaying loans, she thought the less of Martin. This was far from true. She was trying to teach him a set of values and how to look after himself financially, preparing him for the time when she would no longer be around. 'Well, now you're here you may as well eat with me. Cut some bread, son.'

Martin got out a loaf and hacked off four thick slices then they sat down to eat. Saliva filled his mouth as he took the first mouthful of beef stew. The remains from yesterday having been reheated, the flavours had mingled appetisingly. They ate in companionable silence; they were close enough not to feel the need to make inconsequential conversation.

When they had finished Dorothy cleared away the plates and made tea. She wished she knew what was troubling her son.

'Anyone been here?' Martin asked so abruptly that she jumped and the tea leaves on the spoon scattered over the wooden draining-board instead of into the pot.

Dorothy bit her lip. 'No,' she said hesitantly for there were some things she did not want Martin to know, not just yet. 'But Mrs Trevelyan's coming tomorrow. Why?'

'Oh, 'er's all right. I mean anyone else?'

'No. You know only Fred Meecham and Rose come, and Jobber Hicks to give me a lift now and then. What's got into you, Martin?'

'That's all right then.' He avoided an answer but seemed to be relieved as his shoulders unhunched and he pushed back a lock of brown hair. He drank his tea and thanked his mother for the meal then left by the back door, heading up over the rough ground in the direction of his caravan where he intended getting his head down for at least eight hours.

Dorothy remained at the table, her hands clasped around her pint mug as if she was cold. She felt vaguely sick. She had never lied to Martin before. There had been a visitor and she now understood what had brought that particular person to her door. Martin had not been able to keep his mouth shut. However, inadvertently he had done himself a favour and now Dorothy was returning it by keeping quiet.

Outside the night enveloped the house like a cloak. All that could be heard were the familiar creakings of the building. Through the kitchen windows the outlines of boulders became shadowy shapes until they merged completely into the blackness. Clouds hid the stars and there was no streetlighting for a long way. In a couple more days she would need to light a fire. There was a good supply of wood stacked against the side of one of the outbuildings. Martin had cut it for her in the spring and left it there to weather. Fresh wood with the sap still running burnt longer but was no good for giving off heat. Dorothy smiled. She liked the winter when gales made the windows rattle and the wind relentlessly but unsuccessfully pounded away at the house which had stood undamaged for the best part of two hundred years. Only once had she needed someone to come and replace a couple of roof slates.

When the dark evenings arrived Dorothy took herself to bed early and read, her mind always partly aware of the screaming elements outside. When a strong westerly brought rain it lashed against the bedroom window but the sound was comforting, a part of all she had ever known. She would lie contentedly beneath the sheet and blankets and the patchwork quilt her mother had stitched and give thanks for her life.

She was, she realised, a woman of extremes. She liked summer and winter, understood only good or evil and had no time for people who dithered because they couldn't decide the best thing to do. Everything in life was black or white to her and this outlook reflected both her character and her surroundings. She loved the harshness of the scenery outside and could never have lived in one of the picturesque villages which attracted tourists. Even as a girl she had avoided crowds, walking the cliff paths alone or with friends from the village. They would lie amongst the rough grasses and the thrift, its pink flowers bobbing in the soft breezes, and plan their futures, futures modelled on their parents' lives. They knew only open spaces and the moods of the Atlantic Ocean as it battered the coastline or caressed the golden sand. Time was measured by the storms and the baking heat of summer. Their food came from the sea and the surrounding farms, their bread from their mothers' kitchens and their only entertainment was listening to the stories passed down through the generations or hearing one of the choirs sing in the church.

Progress, she thought. What has it brought us but people in a hurry with their fast cars and their televisions and computers which were called, she believed, technology communication? 'Communication!' she spluttered. 'They things does the opposite. Nobody talks any more, not proper. Just tap, tap, tap in they machines. Bleddy tusses.'

She was still at the table, deep in thought, talking aloud as she often did lately. A knock at the door jerked her into alertness. Tap, tap, tap. The sounds were real, not an echo of her thoughts. She was surprised to notice it was now completely dark. 'I'm coming,' she called as she pulled a cardigan around her shoulders and wondered if her visitor had returned.

Peter Pengelly worked on the railways and enjoyed the life although he was not sure how he felt about privatisation. He had recently been promoted to senior conductor on the Inter-City line from Penzance to Paddington although he never completed the whole journey. Mostly the trains changed crews at Plymouth or Exeter. They could manage on what he earned but with two school-age children it wasn't easy, at least according to Gwen.

'Why don't you get a job?' he had asked more than once. 'Just something part-time. You'll probably enjoy it, it'll get you out of the house.'

'I don't want a job, I want to be a proper mother.'

He knew this was not the real reason. Gwen hankered after a life where money was no problem and where she could lord it over others. But she did not want to have to work for it. Sadder still, she had no real friends. Lately he had pressed her harder but she had given him one of her cool glances and made him feel inadequate again.

'There isn't much point now, is there? Your mother won't last for ever. Think about it, Peter, it'll make such a difference to our lives. We can have a bigger house and when all her bits and pieces have been sold—'

'For God's sake,' he had hissed in exasperation, dropping his mug in the washing-up bowl before leaving for work.

'I'll never live out there. Never!' Gwen had shouted after him, almost in tears. All she had ever wanted was a life to make up for her miserable childhood and Dorothy Pengelly was the only thing standing in her way.

That same morning Gwen drove into Truro and bought some new underwear. To her mind Peter was a highly sexed man and she thought she knew exactly how to get what she wanted.

At home, an hour before she was due to collect the children from school, Gwen pulled the flimsy garments out of their plastic carrier and admired them. Her figure was good enough that they would flatter her. Once the children were in bed she would shower and dress in her new things then come downstairs, the lacy garments covered only by her thigh-length robe.

Rose finished the day's work early and returned home at four. The light was blinking on the answering machine. She dropped her camera cases into an armchair and flicked the switch.

'Rose, dear, is that you? It's me, Dorothy. Can you bring some milk with you tomorrow? Oh, be quiet.'

Rose grinned. The short, sharp barks were unmistakably those of George, the Jack Russell. The Greyhound, Star, whose name had been shortened from her racing name of White Star Dancer, did nothing but sleep or rest her lean, greying muzzle on your lap.

'Anyway, if it's not too much trouble. I'll see you all right when you get here.'

Rose knew better than to refuse the money. She had no idea of Dorothy's financial position but had learnt her lesson some time ago when Dorothy had expressed her views on charity. She had, on that same occasion, rather slyly asked Rose's opinion of a painting which hung on her bedroom wall. It was an original Stanhope Forbes and there were, she had hinted, one or two more by various members of the Newlyn School. She had come by them by way of her mother who had mixed with the artists and who had, according to Dorothy, known one or two of them intimately. In those days they had been regarded as bohemian and rather shocking with the women drinking and smoking as well as the men and with their unorthodox lifestyles. Now, of course, they were regarded with admiration. Rose wondered just how intimate the relationships between Dorothy's mother and the painters had been and whether Dorothy might actually be the daughter of one of them.

The picture she had been shown was badly in need of a clean but Rose's experienced eye saw immediately that it was worth a lot of money. It had struck her at the time that this might be Dorothy's way of saying that she could well afford to pay for her shopping. After that incident Rose had taken stock of the contents of Dorothy's house and had realised that amongst the outdated junk there were some good pieces of furniture but her interest in antiques was limited and therefore she had no idea what their value might be. However, it was Dorothy's company she enjoyed, not her possessions. She decided to ring her back.

'It's Rose,' she said when Dorothy finally came to the phone.

'Sorry to keep you, dear, but I was trying to find they blasted cats. Wild, they be, I don't know why I bother with 'un.'

Wild is right, Rose thought, they would as soon scratch and spit as be touched. 'How are you?'

'Fine. A bit tired but the blasted wind kept me awake last night and my shoulder aches. Trouble is, I always fall asleep listening to the radio of an evening then when it's time for bed I toss and turn all night. Makes me teasy, it does. But you don't want to be listening to my moaning.'

Rose frowned. She knew Dorothy refused to consider the possibility that she might be ill. Not once in her life had she been troubled by anything other than minor ailments and she would not give in to them. No doctor had set foot in her house and a midwife had delivered her sons in the wooden-framed bed upstairs.

'How're the grandchildren?'

'Don't see 'em much, really,' Dorothy admitted without self-pity. 'Gwen leads what she calls a busy life, though how that can be with washing-machines and all is beyond me. They're both at school now, and, selfish old woman that I am, I've never volunteered to look after them. Real modern kids they are, into the telly and computer games. They'd be bored silly out here with nothing but fresh air and God's own country all around 'em.'

Rose laughed. She heard the irony in the words. She knew that Dorothy's own children had been content to make their own amusement and had been allowed to run wild over the uninhabited countryside. In his teens Peter had taken to going to friends' houses but Martin had always remained content with his surroundings. Dorothy had shown Rose the treasures she still possessed; small things which Martin had carved out of wood although some of them were unrecognisable as objects.

'Martin's bin drinking more'n's good for him,' Dorothy said as if she had read Rose's mind. 'It's not so much that which bothers me, my husband liked a drop hisself. Ah, well, not much to be done about it. How's that young man of yourn?'

'Jack?' Rose laughed. 'He's not exactly young, and he isn't mine.'

'Got shot of him, have you?' Dorothy cackled down the phone.

'No. We still see each other.'

'Time you was married then. I can't understand you. With me it were all or nothing. Sorry, maid, take no notice of me.'

'It's all right. Really it is.' Dorothy knew that for Rose, too, it was all or nothing. It had been with David. 'I still don't know how I feel about Jack.'

'Early days yet, it's not hardly a year, is it?' Dorothy contradicted herself. 'You'll know, right enough. One day you'll wake up and say he's the right one or he isn't. My, my, listen to that. Can you hear it down your way?'

Rose could. The wind had strengthened and an unexpected rattle of rain hit the window. 'Yes. I hope the electricity doesn't go off again.' It was a common problem. 'I must go, I'll see you tomorrow.'

'I'll look forward to seeing 'e, maid.'

Rose hung up. She could already smell the familiar mixture of dogs and cigarettes and Pear's soap which was Dorothy.

In the attic which she had had converted into a darkroom

Rose developed two rolls of film and left them hanging in the drying cabinet prior to taking prints from them. Jack was coming over. He said he was tired and fancied a quiet night in but he was prepared to provide supper in the form of an Indian takeaway and some alcoholic refreshment Rose had taken pity on him and had offered to cook provided he brought the drinks.

'And will I get to rest my weary head on your pillow?' Jack had half teasingly wanted to know when he rang her. Despite his brashness and his inability to deal with certain matters tactfully he made up for his deficiencies with his offbeat humour and Rose was aware that his show of masculine superiority was only a disguise for his need for reassurance. Jack Pearce, she thought, was as vulnerable as the next man. But do I really want a vulnerable man? was a question she often asked herself.

A crack of thunder made her jump and the rain became a torrent of water which streamed down the side of the house, taking with it mud from the flower beds. The tide was high. By now the waves would be breaking over the Promenade. Rose did not know whether she preferred the vibrant colours and heat of the summer or the violent but spectacular storms of winter.

She showered and washed her hair and changed into a dress, spraying her wrists and neck with perfume which Jack had bought for her last Christmas but which she rarely remembered to use.

Jack could be unpunctual when his job prevented him from being otherwise but tonight he arrived on time, sprinting around the side of the house to the kitchen door, the entrance which all her friends used. She let him in, water dripping from him on to the floor.

'See, I didn't forget.' He kissed the top of her head as he placed a bulging bag bearing the logo of an off-licence on the table. 'Aren't you cold?' He nodded towards her short-sleeved dress.

'Not really.' But soon the dress would be put away for the winter. The evenings were noticeably pulling in and twice in a week she had had to close the bedroom window at night. Jack did look tired but it did not detract from his dark good looks. In jeans and shirt and raincoat, left unbuttoned, his powerful body was shown to advantage. Beside him Rose felt tiny and was never able to get over her surprise at the way in which he seemed to fill a room. But Jack was also trying to fill the life she was building without David. She wasn't quite sure how she had allowed it to happen.

The following morning Rose told Jack she was going to visit Dorothy. 'I'm worried about her. She was a bit pale last time I saw her.'

'Can't you get her GP to call in and see her?'

'I doubt if she's got one. Besides, she'd be furious. God, look at the time. Push off, Jack, I've got loads to do.' He was not on duty until the afternoon but she didn't want him under her feet any longer. She was already regretting letting him stay.

'Is that all the thanks I get for my superb performance last night?'

'Oh, Jack.' He had meant it as a joke but she knew he tried to please her in every way. What was missing was on her side alone.

'I do believe you're blushing, Mrs Trevelyan. I didn't think I'd live to see the day.' He bent to kiss her but something in her eyes warned him not to. 'It's all right, I'm going. Unwillingly, but I'm going. I'll give you a ring later.'

She nodded and watched him leave, his bulk blocking the light from the kitchen window as he passed it.

It was going to be one of those days. No sooner had she washed the dishes which had been left after the previous night's meal than Laura's figure replaced Jack's, although hers was of different dimensions. She too was taller than Rose but thin, naturally so. As she bounced up the path her corkscrew curls bobbed around her shoulders, restricted as they were by a towelling band.

'Don't worry, I won't keep you long,' Laura said, laughing because she had seen Rose's dismayed expression. 'I know you're busy but as I was passing I thought I'd let you know that film we said we'd see is now on in Truro. Fancy going some time?'

Rose did not point out that it would have been easier to telephone but she did understand that on Trevor's first day back at sea Laura felt the need for company. Her three children were grown up and had left home. Two of them had made her a grandmother which, looking at Laura, seemed hard to believe.

'Yes. But not tonight. You might as well put the kettle on now you're here.'

'You obviously had company last night,' Laura said as she nudged Rose out of the way and ran the tap. 'Was it the ever faithful Barry Rowe or the delectable Jack Pearce?'

For the second time that morning Rose blushed. Laura had

not failed to notice that there were two sets of crockery and cutlery on the draining-board and had probably guessed the reason why the dishes had not been seen to until just now.

'No need to answer, your face says it all.' Laura grinned again and creases formed in the tight skin of her face, but instead of ageing her they had the opposite effect. She reminded Rose of an oversized imp.

Rose did not begrudge her the time. Her friend had seen her through the months of David's illness and the awful year which had followed his death. Not once had she told her to pull herself together and she had listened patiently throughout the stage where repetition becomes monotonous and most people get bored. For half an hour they chatted amiably then Laura said she must go.

Bradley Hinkston and Roy Phelps, his associate, had paid a visit to Hayle where they had taken bed and breakfast accommodation at a pub. Two days after their conversation with Martin Pengelly they were on their way back to Bristol where the business was based. Roy was driving the van although Bradley was none too comfortable in the passenger seat, preferring the comfort of his Jaguar.

'It was worth it, then?' Roy took his eyes off the motorway winding ahead of them for a split second. The van had no radio and Roy was not a man at home with silence.

'Oh, yes. It was definitely worth it. The old dear's got a treasure trove there.' From the corner of his eye he saw Roy's thin-lipped smile.

'What's she like? A proper Janner if her son's anything to go by.'

Bradley's arms were crossed. He raised a hand and smoothed his cheek with a forefinger. 'No. Oh, she's got the accent, all right, but I don't think much escapes Mrs Pengelly's notice.'

They had reached the M5 and both were anxious to be back in the city. Since his divorce Roy had lived alone, over the shop, an arrangement convenient to them both and to Bradley's insurers who were pleased to have the rooms over the business occupied. The premises were not the sort that generally passed for an antique shop. There were no oddments of china, no broken chairs and no boxes of junk scattered on the floor. The items he sold were genuine and well cared for. Mostly they consisted of large pieces of furniture along with the occasional bit of porcelain or silver. Everything was displayed under bright lights and there were grilles which pulled down over the windows at night. Roy was never sure if any of Bradley's deals were crooked because he was not privy to them all, like the Pengelly woman, for instance. Still, it was best not to ask. One or two sales a week were enough to keep them both but they usually made far more than that. 'What if she talks?'

'Oh, she won't talk, sunshine, I can guarantee that.'

They reached the outskirts of Bristol and were heading for the centre just as the rain that was sweeping from the west hit them. They drove past Temple Meads Station and continued on to the shop where they unloaded what they had managed to purchase in Cornwall.

'Fancy a drink before I drop you off?'

Bradley nodded as he padlocked the door grille. 'A gin and tonic would go down a treat. I can't be long because I promised the wife I wouldn't be late tonight.' His voice was cultured, his manner urbane. 'All in all a good trip, wouldn't you say?'

Together they walked quickly through the city streets. The shops were closed but the traffic was still heavy. The rain hit the pavements with a steady hiss and the drops bounced up again. They began to walk faster.

After a single gin Bradley glanced at his watch and said it was time he was going. Roy drove him to his house in the suburbs which, he estimated, was worth more than he would ever be able to afford. He bore no grudges because he liked the man with his silvery hair and the twill trousers he favoured who was so very different from himself but who treated him like a father. But he felt unsettled that day. Within him was a sinking feeling that Bradley might have gone over the top back there in Cornwall. He wished he would confide more in him. No, he amended, there had been no need for confidences. Roy knew exactly what Bradley had planned to do.

Bradley's wife welcomed him with an absent-minded kiss on the cheek before carrying on preparing a tray of canapes. 'I won't be long,' she said, 'but you can use the bathroom first.'

Bradley went upstairs anticipating an excellent meal.

As he shaved for the second time that day and got ready to receive their guests he mentally listed the deals he had made during his visit to the West Country and calculated how much money they would make. The Cornish, he thought, are a strange lot. But strangest of all had been the time he had spent in the company of Dorothy Pengelly.

CHAPTER THREE

Rose intended making a start on the wild flower sketches after she had seen Dorothy. She drove out of Penzance and joined the dual carriageway, taking a left at the roundabout.

The rain had eased off but the road was still wet and drops of moisture clung to the long grass in the verges, glittering in the sunshine. Behind her was St Michael's Mount, Rose caught a glimpse of it in her rear mirror, and around her was countryside. It would be a nice day after all. But something was wrong, Rose knew it. David had once said she was more superstitious than the Cornish and that her sixth sense was developed enough for her to be classed as one of them. Please let him be wrong, she prayed as she neared Dorothy's house.

There was no ferocious barking from George as she swung into the drive nor did Dorothy come to the door at the sound of the Mini's engine. A car passed on the main road, but other than that there was silence. Not even a bird sang. Anxiety gripped her as she approached the front door. On the grass to one side of her a crow, busy shredding something with its beak, paused to glance at her then hopped a few paces away before flying off. The front door was slightly ajar. Rose stopped, her heart beating faster. She could hear something now, some faint sound coming from within the house. It might have been someone in pain. At least she would be able to do something about it if Dorothy had fallen over. She knocked and called out but there was no response. Pushing open the door she called again. 'Dorothy? It's me. Rose.'

The sounds were coming from the kitchen. Rose hurried towards them then stood in the doorway trying to make sense of the scene before her. Dorothy lay on the floor, her head cradled in Martin's lap. It was Martin she had heard. He was gently rocking his mother and making crooning noises as tears ran down his face. Star was asleep in her basket and George, normally so volatile, whimpered quietly, curled up in Dorothy's armchair.

'What's happened? What's happened to her?' Martin asked Rose, seeming unsurprised to see her there.

'I don't know, Martin. Have you called an ambulance?'

He shook his head. Rose quickly took over. She bent over Dorothy and touched her. She was stone cold and her eyes were slits, the half-moons of her irises dull. Dorothy Pengelly was dead. Rose knew that at once. It was too late for an ambulance but she was not qualified to presume that. She rang for one anyway. Mike Phillips, she thought, Mike who had cared for David, he would tell her what she ought to do. No wonder Dorothy had been pale the other day, she had obviously been ill. Too late, Rose wished she had taken Jack's advice and sent a doctor anyway.

One of the hospital switchboard operators bleeped Mike

43

and he came to the phone quickly, knowing that Rose would not disturb him unless it was necessary.

'Mike. My friend . . . Dorothy . . . oh, Mike, she's dead.'

'Stay calm, Rose. Have you rung for an ambulance?'

'Yes.'

'Who's her GP?'

'She doesn't have one.'

'Look, I think you ought to call the police as well. The paramedics'll probably do it anyway. If she's always been fit the police surgeon will want to take a look at her.'

'Thanks, Mike.' Rose replaced the receiver feeling stupid to have telephoned but it had been reassuring just speaking to him.

Martin had not moved, he was still rocking Dorothy. She wondered whether she ought to make him some strong sweet tea but felt a sense of repugnance at the idea of moving around Dorothy's kitchen and using her things whilst she lay there on the floor.

It seemed a long time until she heard a vehicle turn into the driveway although it could not have been more than a few minutes. The police arrived first. She had contacted Camborne station as it was the nearest.

One of the PCs made a quick examination of Dorothy and nodded to his colleague who turned away and spoke into his lapel radio. Martin ignored them all.

'Are you a relative?'

Rose shook her head. 'A friend. Martin's her son.'

They all stared at him. 'There'll be a doctor here soon. I think the lad needs attention too.'

The ambulance arrived, its siren shattering the subdued

silence. The crew assessed the situation and saw that their services were unnecessary.

By the time the police surgeon had joined them the kitchen was crowded. 'There'll need to be a PM,' he told Rose, realising that Martin was in no state to take in anything. 'I'll arrange for her body to be collected. Is there anywhere Martin can go?'

'He can come back with me.'

'Good. And I suggest you get his GP to have a look at him.'

Rose nodded. It would have to be her own. He could not be left alone now and she could not begin to think what the loss of his mother would do to him.

'We'll need to ask you some questions,' one of the officers said. 'And Mr Pengelly in due course.'

There was little Rose could tell them. She described the scene as she had come upon it and they were told they could leave. 'What did she die from?' Rose asked.

'I'm not sure. Heart maybe?' The surgeon shrugged. He wasn't sure but there was a smell of alcohol and an empty paracetamol bottle which one of the police officers had picked up and shown him discreetly. The post-mortem would show if his suspicions were correct. It was not for him to blab to all and sundry that Dorothy Pengelly had taken her own life.

With the help of one of the policemen she got Martin to his feet. Taking his arm she led him out to the car. Tall and big-boned as he was, he allowed himself to be gently settled into the front passenger seat. Rose took a quick look at him as she started the engine. His dark hair grew long over his collar, his face was tear-stained and his brown eyes were unseeing but Rose did not think he would do something stupid, like trying to jump out of the car while it was moving. 'Martin?' she tried tentatively, touching his arm. 'We're going back to my place. You can stay the night with me.' Her voice was firmer now. She had to take control, not let her own grief surface until she was sure Martin was all right. There were still some of David's things in the airing cupboard, it was ironic that it had taken another death for them to be put to use. Driving home she was glad that they would not be there to see Dorothy's body taken away.

When Martin finally spoke his words frightened Rose. 'She'll all right soon, won't she?' he asked, making it clear that he had no idea of the finality of it.

'She's dead, Martin,' Rose said quietly, but she could not bring herself to say that she would never be coming back. Once they were safely at home she would try to get through to him.

She parked on the small concrete patch at the top of the path alongside the house and let them in. In her handbag were Dorothy's spare keys which the police had told her to take as someone would need to feed the animals. She had told them that Martin lived elsewhere and that there was another son who needed to be informed. Thankfully, that would not be her job. As she placed the keys on top of the fridge tears filled her eyes. Shock had worn off and she felt the loss of her friend badly. With her back to Martin she waited until she was more in control until she turned to face him. She had noticed there were four keys on the ring, two Yale, two Chubb, and realised that she had two identical sets. Presumably Peter would have a third.

Tomorrow the police wanted to question Martin. Rose

owed it to Dorothy to ensure that he was ready and able to face up to their questions. She pulled out a chair and sat next to him.

'Peter,' he said before she had a chance to begin. 'You have to tell Peter.'

Rose nodded. It was a good sign. He understood that his brother needed to know which meant he was aware that something was dreadfully wrong. 'The police will go and see him, there's nothing to worry about.' Useless words, Rose knew better than most. But there were no words which could ease the pain or change the situation. 'Would you like something to drink?' Dorothy had mentioned her anxiety on this count but these were exceptional circumstances. She barely remembered the three days after David's funeral when she had locked herself in the house, refusing to answer the door or the telephone as she sat drinking one bottle of wine after another, unwashed and without food. The long months of nursing and the final days spent at the hospital had taken their toll. Only then did she allow herself the indulgence of obliteration. It was Laura who had finally shouted at her through the letterbox, saying that if she didn't open the door she'd break the bloody thing down. If Martin now needed the temporary comfort of alcohol she would not deny him it.

'I'd like some tea, please. Can I smoke?'

'Of course you can.' She got out the only ashtray she possessed and placed it on the table. Rose smoked occasionally but no longer got through a packet a day. As she made the tea with shaking hands she wondered if Dorothy had left a will. As far as she was aware there were no relatives other than her two sons. It was an uncharitable thought but she hoped that Peter and his wife did not hold another set of keys because she suspected they might remove anything of value before probate had been finalised.

Impossible to work now. Even if she'd been up to it Martin needed someone to be with him. He was, she realised as she placed his tea before him, the same size as Jack but he appeared to have shrunk somehow.

Catching sight of her wristwatch she saw it was already mid-afternoon. Without asking if he was hungry Rose made some sandwiches but Martin did little more than take a few mouthfuls and crumble the bread between his fingers. His grief was plain to see but he seemed ill at ease. Rose watched him as she tried to eat her own sandwich. She had a habit of skipping meals and recently her jeans had become looser. She kicked off her canvas shoes and hooked her hair behind her ears. She must eat to encourage Martin although she gagged on the bread, and then she had to get him to talk.

Without warning he stood up. 'I think I killed her,' he said. 'I want to go home.'

At that moment the telephone rang. 'Sit down, Martin. I won't be a minute.' Rose went to answer it, too dazed to think straight. It was Doreen Clarke, a woman she had met some time ago when she had been commissioned to take photographs of the house of a wealthy family. Doreen cleaned other people's houses and was a great source of gossip, a pastime for which she was renowned. But surely even Doreen couldn't have heard the news yet?

'Rose, dear,' she began, 'I was wondering if you'd open the Christmas bazaar for us this year? I know it isn't until December but you can't leave these things until the last minute. Only, you see, we tried to get whatshisname, the MP, but he's got other commitments and we can't find anyone else who's willing.'

Despite everything Rose felt a flicker of amusement. The two women's initial dislike of each other had mellowed and turned into mutual respect until they had finally become friends. Doreen now considered her to be a minor celebrity but it was apparent that she was by no means first choice for the job. 'What's the date?' Rose flicked through her diary knowing that she had nothing booked that far ahead. 'Yes, that's fine. But I hope people won't be disappointed, I'm sure no one will know who I am.'

'Of course they will,' Doreen assured her firmly. 'I'll make sure your name's on all the posters and in the adverts in the paper. Here, why don't you bring along some of your stuff? You might make a sale or two?'

'I'll think about it. Doreen, I've got a visitor at the moment, I'll have to go. Thanks for asking me.' Rose replaced the receiver and went back to the kitchen. Martin hadn't moved. He remained standing behind his chair, his large-knuckled hands gripping the back of it, his eyes staring. For a second Rose wondered if he was mad.

'I don't think you ought to be alone, Martin. Why not stay here tonight?'

'Please, Mrs Trevelyan, I want to go home.'

'I'll drive you, but first you must tell me what you mean.' Martin was frightened. Perhaps Dorothy had still been alive when he found her and he now realised he ought to have called for help.

'I told 'un.'

'Told who, Martin? I don't understand you.'

49

'The men.'

'What men?' She couldn't guess how the police would deal with him.

'In the pub.' He clamped his mouth shut. 'I want to go home.'

Rose hesitated then nodded. He was in shock, he didn't know what he was talking about. Dorothy had told her how he drank too much, it was highly unlikely he'd remember anything he'd said to someone in the pub. Assessing him she saw that perhaps he was better on his own. Men like him, used to solitude and uncomfortable in other people's homes, would heal quicker if left alone. Tomorrow she would go and talk to him again.

Reluctantly she drove him back, praying that she was doing the right thing. Martin had been so close to his mother that she feared for his state of mind. If anything happened to him it would be on her conscience for ever. Already she had ignored the advice to get a doctor to see him. It would be pointless, a doctor couldn't bring Dorothy back, nor could he ease Martin's pain. All he could do was prescribe pills to blot it out temporarily. Besides, she tried to reassure herself, she could not force a grown man to remain under her roof.

The working day was coming to a close and the traffic heading in the opposite direction was building up. Although there was little on her side of the road she got stuck behind a tractor piled high with bales of hay. It turned sharply into a farm gateway, the rear end of the trailer swinging behind it. The clouds were moving faster, building up from the west until they were banked in a grey mass. Rose wound up the window as the wind changed direction. On the slopes the heather was beginning to flower. Walking through it, hand in hand, were a couple. Had Martin ever had a girlfriend? she wondered. It would have been nice if there was someone other than herself to comfort him. She doubted his brother and his wife would trouble themselves.

Stopping as near to the caravan as she was able she watched him climb slowly up over the rough ground, his head bowed, his arms hanging limply at his sides. She had no idea what was going on in his head. For a second she had a maternal urge to run after him and hold him tightly but it would embarrass them both. When he had disappeared over the brow of the hill she turned the Mini around and went home to find another message on her answering machine. It was Barbara Phillips, the wife of Mike Phillips whom she had rung earlier in the day. 'Rose, are you there? Never mind. It's me, Barbara. Mike told me what happened. You poor thing. Give me a ring when you can. Look, I know this isn't a good time but I'm having a bit of a do to celebrate Mike's fiftieth. Saturday week. You've got to be here, and I won't take no for an answer. Ring me when you can. We'll be thinking of you.' Dear Barbara, who had during that awful year gently but persistently encouraged her to go out more but who now did so forcefully. Here was a chance to meet new people. I'll go, Rose thought. Alone. No Jack and no Barry.

Barry. Suddenly she remembered that she was supposed to be meeting him that evening for a long-standing dinner date. She would not ring him to cancel, it would be too hard breaking the news over the telephone. Let him come, then she would tell him.

There were three appointments in her diary for the next

day. Rose did cancel them. Tomorrow she must make sure Martin was all right and she needed time for herself, time to grieve for Dorothy. It had not really hit her yet. Aimlessly, she wandered around the house which she loved and where she had always been so happy. What had happened to her youthful dreams? Was the woman who drew and painted wild flowers and pretty bays for commercial purposes the same girl who had had such high hopes for herself? Having gained a place at art college and having been told she had talent, her ambition had been to make a living in oils; wild, dramatic oils of rugged seascapes and rocky promontories. After a brief flirtation with contemporary art she knew it was not for her. Rose's work was representational, alive and real.

She hadn't given herself a chance. Just because her initial attempts had not created a storm didn't mean she could not have improved. Few artists were instantly recognised, many not at all. Up until David had died she had painted one or two oils each year, after his death there had been only one. And now Dorothy's death had shown her how tenuous the grip on life was. It was time she made some changes.

Jobber Hicks had been farming since the day he left school at fourteen and by that time had already completed his apprenticeship by way of the various tasks he was allocated each evening and which he did as soon as he had changed out of his uniform. Only then could he wash and sit down at the table with the rest of the family and eat the large meal his mother prepared for them every day. Of the five children he was the only one who had remained on the farm. When his father died he had taken over his role. By that time his mother had been dead for five years.

The money that Harry Hicks had scrupulously saved had been divided equally between the children but Jobber's three sisters and brother showed no interest in making any claim on the farm itself. They were all married and comfortable in their different ways and they knew that if the property was sold Jobber would be out of work and have nowhere to go. They were not interested in a fifth of its worth because the whole place had fallen into disrepair since Mrs Hicks's death and the land surrounding it belonged to the Duchy anyway. The deeds were transferred to Jobber and he began the long task of renovating the farm.

Jobber was also the only one to remain single. From his youth he had always hankered after Dorothy Pengelly, or Trelawny, as she had been then. She was different from the other girls he knew, having guts and spirit from an early age. When her husband died his hopes were renewed. He waited for a decent interval then began to woo her in his own steady way. Dorothy disappointed him by saying that she had no intention of marrying again, one husband had been enough. Jobber never knew how close to saying yes she had been. He had had to content himself with the farm and her friendship but he had wanted more.

His work usually took up ten or more hours a day so he employed a married woman to come in and cook and clean. During school holidays she would bring her small daughter whom Jobber would sometimes take out with him. He was touched by her devotion and by the way she would slip her hand in his without prompting.

He had been christened Joseph Robert Hicks but when

Florrie, the baby of the family, first began to speak she could not master his names and ran them into one. Jobber, she had called him and the name had stuck.

He sat in the kitchen in an armchair beside the range which burnt all year to serve the back-boiler and the ovens. He was ashamed, he could not remember when he had last cried, but Dorothy's death had rocked his world. His own mortality did not bother him, death would come at some point and occasionally it seemed welcome. But how he would miss those jaunts into Camborne and being able to go up to the house and discuss all manner of things with her. The last time he had seen her he had had the strong impression there was something she wanted to tell him.

He thought of Martin. As soon as Rose had rung him he had driven over but the boy was neither at the house nor in his van. Mid-evening he had found him, sitting on a rock, the setting sun giving his pale face a rosy glow. He had barely responded to Jobber's questions.

Jobber dried his eyes and pulled out his pipe, sucking at the stem and spitting out the sticky blackness which lined it before tamping the bowl with strong-smelling tobacco. Once it was lit he applied himself to the question of Dorothy's younger son. He decided to go and see him and ask if he might have Star, the Greyhound. It would be nice to have something of Dorothy's to which she had been attached. Niggling at the back of his mind was the worry that he had put too much pressure on her. If it was heart trouble the last thing she needed was his persistent efforts to get her to marry him.

CHAPTER FOUR

'What do you say, Peter?' Gwen stood with her hands on her hips, her head on one side, waiting for an answer. She had already half extracted a promise that he would sell his mother's house when the time came. Her husband slowly chewed a piece of toast, his face as yet unshaven, as he sat at the kitchen table where all their meals were taken because they did not have a dining-room.

'It sounds like a reasonable idea, but she'll not agree.'

'You don't know unless you ask.' Gwen sat down, her elbows on the table as she leant forward enthusiastically. She did not tell Peter that she had been up to see Dorothy, nor could she ever admit what had happened. 'Look, it might be just what she's waiting for. You know how proud she is, she'll never admit she can't cope up there by herself. I bet she's just waiting for you to suggest it. Besides, she'll be far better off in one of those warden-controlled places.'

Peter was not prepared to argue so for the sake of peace he agreed to put the proposition to his mother although he knew the outcome in advance. Gwen had changed her tune, she was, by her standards, talking quite reasonably. But something was wrong, he could tell by the excitement in her eyes. Excitement? Or was it agitation? He never really knew what was going on in his wife's mind. He supposed that she imagined his mother would simply hand over the money. In which case she was a fool. The state would want the proceeds of the sale for taking care of her.

'She's never spent a penny on any of us – she's selfish, you know that. We could do with the money while we're young enough to enjoy it.'

'That's enough! I've said I'll mention it, now leave it.' He shook his head in exasperation. He was still a young man with a young family but Gwen was wearing him out and today he couldn't fathom her at all. Still slagging his mother off but without the usual venom, almost like a cat that's had the cream, he thought, resorting to clichés because he was unable to think straight when his wife's behaviour confused him.

Satisfied that she had done all she could, that she had covered her tracks, she slipped a hand inside Peter's shirt and massaged his chest. The children had been dropped at school by a friend, there was time enough to go back upstairs before Peter had to leave for work.

Later, when Gwen was about to collect them from school, she saw, from her bedroom window, the police car pull up. 'Oh, God,' she whispered as the two officers got out and approached her door. 'What have I done?'

Ashen-faced and with trembling legs she made it down the stairs just as they rang the bell.

'Mrs Pengelly?'

Gwen nodded, unable to speak, her fingers clutching at the buttons of her dress.

'May we come in?'

'Yes.' Her voice was hoarse.

PC Tregidgo ushered his female companion ahead of him. It was she, as Gwen had expected, who said that Dorothy was dead. Gwen's legs finally gave out. Her knees buckled and she slumped back into an armchair. The WPC offered to make tea.

'No. No, thanks, I'm fine. Really. It was just such a shock. I mean, she was old, I knew it would happen at some time, but, well, you never do really expect it, do you?' She was babbling and she knew it. 'My children. I've got to fetch them from school.'

'Can't a neighbour go? I really don't think you ought to drive. Can we ring someone?'

Gwen capitulated. She, too, thought it doubtful that she'd be able to control the foot pedals. PC Tregidgo also rang the school to let them know that someone else would be collecting the Pengelly children.

'What did she die of?'

'We don't know yet for certain. There'll be a post-mortem.'

'Oh, I see.'

The two officers exchanged a glance. Most people were upset when they heard this news, Mrs Pengelly's daughter-in-law actually seemed pleased. An empty paracetamol bottle did not necessarily prove that the old lady had swallowed the lot, she may simply have taken the last two because of chest pains for all they knew. It was up to the pathologist to find out. For the moment their instructions were that the cause of death was as yet unknown.

'Can we go ahead with any arrangements?'

'I'm afraid not, not until after the inquest.'

'Inquest. Yes, I see.' Gwen pressed her lips firmly together. In a minute she'd lose control, she'd felt her teeth knocking when she relaxed her jaw. 'And the post-mortem, why's that necessary?'

'It's quite normal under the circumstances if someone dies suddenly and they're not under medical supervision.'

'Yes. Good.'

PC Tregidgo raised his eyebrows and tilted his head towards the kitchen. The WPC took the hint and went to put the kettle on. Mrs Pengelly seemed to be in shock, her reactions were not those they usually experienced in such cases.

'What time'll your husband be home?'

Gwen looked up. The policeman did seem young, it was true what they said. 'Not until about ten. He works for Great Western.'

'Is there someone who can sit with you?'

'No. I'll be fine, and I'll have the children.'

By the time they had drunk the tea the children had returned home, dropped by one of the neighbours. They were unnaturally quiet at the sight of the two uniforms and went upstairs to their rooms.

Alone at last Gwen went straight to the kitchen cupboard and pulled out a bottle of whisky. She half filled a tumbler and drank most of it standing by the sink. It was an unprecedented action but never more needed. Five minutes later she started to prepare tea for Kirsty and Michael. Breathing deeply to steady herself she realised that now she would be able to buy some more dresses. She never wore jeans or trousers, they were unfeminine and she knew what men liked. Better still, they could move to a large house. But first she had to deal with the guilt and the fear.

Rose was staring out of the window; her face was wet with tears so she did not immediately notice it was raining, 'Oh, Dorothy,' she said sadly. 'How I'm going to miss you.' She brushed at her face impatiently and went to the kitchen and out into the garden to retrieve the washing which flapped furiously in the spray-laden wind and rain. Hurriedly she unpegged it and threw it into the basket. From the comparative warmth of the kitchen she could hear the loose brass knob on her bedroom door rattling because the windows were open.

As she placed the washing basket on the table a wave of exhaustion swept over her. Delayed reaction. As long as there had been Martin to consider her own feelings hadn't come into it. And now she was dreading telling Barry Rowe. Rose could not see that Dorothy's death was that simple. Yes, she was old and not quite as strong as she liked to think, but she was tough and she hadn't shown any of the symptoms of heart disease. Yes, Rose knew it could happen, a sudden massive coronary, but not to Dorothy, surely? Barry would struggle to hide his annoyance because he was always angry when she became too involved with other people. Jealous, more like, she thought. But Barry Rowe and Jack Pearce no longer seemed to matter much. At some point during that apparently fruitful staring out of the window she had made up her mind about her future.

With a glass of wine in her hand she waited in the sitting-room in her favourite armchair for Barry to arrive. The suite was covered in fading chintz, there was an open fire, lit in the winter to supplement the central heating, and cosy table lamps, and nothing was quite straight. Rose's house, like its detached neighbours, was built of Cornish granite and the rooms were small, although comfortable. The floors sloped imperceptibly and the walls were uneven. Upstairs they were emulsioned but the sitting-room walls remained in their original state, the glittering granite cold but enduring. On the floor was a deep claret carpet which continued through the hall and up the stairs.

Restless, Rose picked up their framed wedding photograph and studied it, unable to understand how she still felt mentally as young as the girl who smiled back at her. Like Dorothy she did not think she would remarry but she had not ruled it out entirely. Sometimes Jack stayed overnight but she could not envisage living with him on a permanent basis. There was a frisson between them which could lead to laughter or, equally, to an argument, but that wasn't enough. And if she was honest, the novelty was wearing off. She replaced the photograph as she heard Barry calling from the kitchen.

'Oh, Rosie, I don't know what to say.' Barry Rowe stood in the kitchen looking so pitiful that Rose almost laughed. His thinning hair was damp and so were the shoulders of his jacket. His glasses were misted with rain and had slipped down his nose and he seemed not to know what to do with his hands.

'Some wine?' Rose poured him a glass, aware that he had wanted to reach out and put his arms around her, but they rarely had any physical contact. 'I don't feel like going out, I hope you don't mind.'

'Of course I don't. You should've rung me.' He watched her slender figure as she moved around the kitchen. In jeans and T-shirt, her hair tied back untidily, she hardly looked more than a child. Jack Pearce or not, he thought, he wouldn't have stood a chance.

'I can't believe she just died like that.' Rose raised her hands, palms uppermost in disbelief. 'I mean, not Dorothy.'

'No one ever believes it at first.' Barry stopped. He had been about to add, 'You should know better than most.'

'Well, it'll be interesting to hear the result of the post-mortem.'

'You've got to stop doing this, Rose.'

'Doing what?'

She spun around to face him, irritation making her tone sharper than she had intended. Unless she slapped him down now and then Barry had a tendency to be dictatorial.

'Getting involved.' He shrugged. 'Finding problems where there are none.'

'I thought the world of Dorothy, you don't know how much I'll miss her.' She felt the tears starting again. 'And just because you don't give a damn about the human race doesn't mean we're all the same.'

'I'm sorry, Rose. I think it's best if I go now.'

'So do I.' Rigidly she watched him leave, pulling his jacket collar up against the rain, then she sank into a chair. Poor Barry, she thought. He had never been close to anyone. Orphaned young and with no siblings he had been unable to form real relationships. His total emotional output was expended upon herself and she had been mean to him. How could she expect him to understand that she and Dorothy had been kindred spirits? Both had lost their husbands and through their losses had grown into strong, independent women. Rose knew how fiercely she protected this independence. Whatever Barry thought, she knew there was something wrong. And then the real pain began. 'Oh, David, oh, Dorothy,' she gasped before laying her head in her arms on the table and sobbing.

Rose woke at six unable to recall going to bed. Sleep had not revived her, she felt listless and depressed. Outside the rain continued to pour down, drenching everything and bouncing off the glass roof of the porch. In a way she was sorry she had cancelled her appointments.

Trying to make use of her time she spent the morning in the darkroom developing and printing several rolls of film. At a little after midday Jack rang. He, too, sounded tired.

'I would've rung last night but I thought you'd rather be left alone.'

'Thanks, Jack.' Of course he would know about Dorothy. It was to Camborne that she had telephoned.

'Want me to come over?'

'No.' She did not offer any explanation.

'Rose?'

She waited, knowing by the tone of his voice that there was more to come, that he hadn't only telephoned to see how she was.

'Rose, the post-mortem took place today. The path bloke wasn't busy so he fitted it in.'

'And?'

'And . . . Well, the final results aren't available yet . . . Look, this is confidential until after the inquest, OK?'

'You don't need to ask, Jack.'

'No. I'm sorry. Dorothy committed suicide.'

'Don't be ridiculous.' Rose was actually laughing.

'The stomach contents say so. An overdose. There was an empty paracetamol bottle at the scene and—'

'At the scene? Come off it, Jack, it's me you're talking to. Not in a million years would Dorothy kill herself, she loved life too much.'

'It wasn't paracetamol.'

'All right, what was it then?'

'Something stronger. We don't know yet. She confided in you, was anything worrying her?'

'She didn't kill herself so just sod off.' Rose hung up.

Fred Meecham drove away from the hospital in a state of numbness finally acknowledging that Marigold was going to die.

Lying in the high bed, her skin grey against the white sheets, emaciated and almost fading away before his eyes, she had seemed like someone else, someone he had not met before.

He was so preoccupied with Marigold that the realisation that Dorothy Pengelly had been found dead hardly touched him. As he parked the van behind the shop he began to think of her, wishing, too late, that he had heeded her advice instead of carrying on unrealistically. Throughout his life Fred had been unaware that his own actions could affect others. He lived in a world where he believed things were done *to* him, that he was moulded and altered by external events, rather than having any influence over his own destiny By nature he was insecure. Until Marigold came back into his life his only comfort had been in God. But Marigold had changed everything and for the first time in his life he had acted out of character. Fred could not see that if people knew of some of the things he had done before she had come to live with him, they would consider them to be so unlike him as to be impossible.

Upstairs in the flat he sat in the darkness. The wind was rising, the trees at the back swaying, their leaves shaking off droplets of water as the glow from the streetlight flickered between them. Soon it would be winter, really and metaphorically. Without Marigold there could be no spring or summer. There was no hope, nothing to assuage the loss he had coming. All Fred had ever wanted was a faithful companion, someone to share his life, someone who would not let him down like all the others. Marigold had been that person, worthy of all the love he had to give. They had, he saw, saved each other. There wasn't a customer who didn't declare what a devoted brother and sister they were. Now she, too, was leaving him and there was nothing he could do to stop it happening.

As he tried to come to terms with the future he realised that the past did still matter. He had imagined that once he was alone again he would not care. Instead of wishing himself dead, hoping that he, too, could join Marigold as quickly as possible, a strong sense of survival was emerging and, with it, a need to protect everything he had fought so hard to attain.

Some time during the small hours he took himself to bed. He slept uneasily and dreamt of Dorothy. It was her he saw in that hospital bed, not Marigold. There was blood on the sheets, seeping slowly and brightly down across the counterpane, but Dorothy was smiling, mocking him. Clutched in her hands were bundles of fifty-pound notes, around her were his customers making the same sounds they made in his shop, muttering the same banalities, avoiding the word cancer as if it was contagious. 'How is she?' they would whisper as if by speaking quietly they could lessen the horror. He saw in their faces pity and sympathy but also relief that it wasn't themselves or one of their own who was suffering.

In the dream they, too, mocked him as if they could see into his soul and knew the secrets hidden there. Everyone seemed to be there, huddled around that bed, standing or sitting, admiring the flowers on the locker, yet still there was room for the nurses and the doctor who came rushing to Dorothy's bedside as a long, soft 'Oooh' was breathed in unison. Dorothy had flung the bloodstained money at Fred before falling back, her mouth open as she died. Rose Trevelyan stood at the head of the bed, smiling.

The money floated weightlessly above their heads like confetti taken by the wind. His customers reached up, trying to grab it, ignoring Fred who became aware that he was invisible. They were as one; he was, as always, on the outside. He walked through the heaving mass of bodies without feeling contact.

When he woke he was sweating although a chill breeze blew through the window he had forgotten to close. His mouth was dry and it took him several seconds to realise that it was a dream and that, although Dorothy had really died, Marigold was still alive, but he rang the hospital just to make sure.

He prayed as he dressed: Please, God, not today, don't take her away from me yet. As he fastened his tie he nodded slowly as if responding to some unheard voice. Good. It wouldn't be today.

The bathroom cabinet seemed bare now since the hospital had asked him to bring in all of Marigold's medication when she was admitted. There had been so much of it as the long days passed. He had kept it there although it was not as convenient as beside her bed but he didn't want her room to look like a sick room. By her bed had been flowers and a pile of the romantic novels she liked to read. Only she hadn't read much lately, her arms were too weak to hold the books. Fred had gone back to the library and exchanged them for paperbacks. Marigold had smiled and thanked him and had finally explained that she couldn't see too well. Each day added to the burden of her infirmities and the doctor had told him it was only a matter of time.

'How long?' Fred had asked.

'Days. Maybe less.'

He was going straight there. Days. Fred wanted every second with her. When it was over would be the time to think about the other things, to think about what Dorothy had said. But Dorothy was dead; when Marigold died too he would be the only one who knew.

CHAPTER FIVE

Like most people, Doreen Clarke learnt of Dorothy's death within twenty-four hours and spread the news as quickly as she had come to hear of it. On Sunday she was going to visit her sister in the village of Paul and Rose had invited her around for coffee first. Gossip though she was, Doreen was tempted to cancel the arrangement because, knowing how close to Dorothy Rose had been, she did not want to be the one to break the news if she hadn't already heard. It was her husband, Cyril, who talked some sense into her, saying she could not turn her back on a friend and, besides, young Jack Pearce would've put her wise.

Rose was ironing when she arrived. It was one of those deceptively warm September days when it seemed as if summer was beginning rather than ending. A vivid blue sky arched high over Mount's Bay, framing the Mount itself. Beneath it the sea shimmered as silver ripples skimmed its surface. Ozone hung in the air with the ever-present tang of fish. Even the gulls were quiet.

Rose had the back door open; her face was flushed with

the heat of the iron. She was dressed in faded jeans and a T-shirt. Doreen studied her for a second, aware of how much younger than herself Rose looked although there was less than a year's difference in their ages. Doreen favoured sensible skirts and jumpers and her straight grey hair was cut level with her chin.

The kitchen was filled with the aromas of domesticity, of coffee and clean cotton clothes, the starchy steam of the iron and the toast Rose had made herself eat earlier.

'Come in, Doreen. I'm glad you're here, I hate this job.'

'Don't we all,' Doreen replied as Rose unplugged the iron. She saw at once that Rose knew. Her friend's face was drawn and there were dark circles beneath eyes which had recently shed tears. Doreen clutched her large black handbag to her stomach with both hands as if for protection. 'So you've heard about Dorothy. Poor old thing, I could hardly take it in.'

'Yes, I know. I was there. On Friday. I brought Martin back with me but he didn't want to stay. He was here when you rang, actually.' Rose chewed a thumbnail hoping that Doreen was not offended.

Doreen nodded. She did not need further explanation, she could imagine how upset Rose would have been. 'Poor lamb. Real fond of his mother, he was. I wonder what'll happen to him now? Still, the other one'll be pleased, no doubt. Probably rubbing his hands with delight, if you ask me.'

'Have a seat, Doreen, for goodness' sake.' Rose busied herself with cups and saucers. Doreen knew the Pengellys better than Rose did because she lived in Hayle herself, but Rose did not want to discuss them, nor did she mention that

Jack had been pumping her for reasons why Dorothy might have killed herself. Doreen could read it for herself in the *Cornishman* after the inquest.

'That Gwen thinks she's better'n all of us, got her heart set on a big house, that one has. I hope she's disappointed, that's all I can say. Fat lot of attention she paid her mother-in-law when she was alive, I don't rightly know if she even took the kids out to see her. Wouldn't surprise me if Dorothy left the lot to a dogs' home. Serve 'er right, it would.'

Dropping a sweetener into her cup and placing the sugar bowl on the table for Doreen, Rose was barely listening. She could have predicted the conversation. All she knew, all she instinctively felt, was that the police report was wrong. But what could she do about it?

'I've heard she'd got a few good bits and pieces up there,' Doreen continued confidentially, leaning forward to speak as if there was a chance of being overheard. 'Well, you'd know more about that than me, you being an artist and all. Wouldn't surprise me if that Gwen doesn't go up there and help herself because I don't suppose Martin realises what her stuff's worth.'

Coming from Doreen it sounded callous but the same thought had crossed Rose's mind, although Martin had reassured her when she dropped him home. 'Ma had three sets of keys. I've got one. I'll need it to feed the dogs.' So, surprisingly, Rose was in possession of the only other keys. Had Peter not been trusted with them? He had not contacted her to ask for a set and she was glad if what Doreen said was correct. It's none of your business, she chided herself and offered Doreen more coffee by way of changing the subject.

As they drank it Doreen caught Rose eyeing the ironing still waiting to be done.

'It's all right, dear. Violet's expecting me any time and she gets in a right to-do if the dinner's served up late. I'll be on my way if I can get the car out of the drive. I don't know how you do it.' Doreen patted her hand. 'Give me a ring later.'

Rose watched her rounded figure plod down the path and out to where she had parked the ancient vehicle which took her from one cleaning job to another. Apart from Cyril's pension it had been their only income since the mines had closed. With a sigh Rose picked up the iron. No sooner had she finished one blouse than a shadow fell across her. It was Jack.

'Can I come in?' He looked sheepish.

'Yes. If you want coffee help yourself. I'm awash with it.'

He did so and sat down, uninvited. 'Look, Rose, I apologise if I upset you, but are you really convinced she wouldn't kill herself?'

'One hundred per cent.'

Jack stretched out his long legs and stroked his chin. 'We'll have to wait for the inquest but we're making discreet inquiries.'

'Oh?' Rose continued ironing, annoyed that he should turn up unannounced.

'Mm, very discreet because there was no sign of forced entry and from all accounts nothing seems to have been taken. Her purse was there with money in it and . . .'

Rose stood still. 'You mean you believe me?'

'I'm not saying that, I'm simply saying that nothing points to it being anything other than suicide except that she wasn't registered with any local doctor and it wasn't paracetamol which she swallowed. And it seems a bit extravagant to find a doctor out of the area if you intend taking your own life because there're enough drugs behind the counter of any chemist's shop to do the trick.'

'So?'

'So, is there any chance of you nosing around? You know the family.'

'I see. Once more I'm supposed to do your job for you.' She flung her hair back over her shoulder angrily.

'Oh, Rose, you're always so defensive. I thought you'd be pleased. Do as you wish. I really came here to see if I could buy you a drink. I thought you'd need cheering up.'

He is very handsome, Rose thought, and I'm attracted to him, but if he can irritate me this much now, how much worse would it be if the relationship were more serious? She unplugged the iron, wondering if the job would ever be done. 'All right then, but somewhere local.'

'The Star?'

'The Star's fine.'

They made no overt signs of affection in public, it would have been out of character for them both. Instead they strolled down the narrow pavement of the hill in single file, stopping for a minute to watch a fishing-boat turn in through the mouth of the harbour. There was a cat's cradle of masts alongside the north pier and the smell of fish was stronger there.

The bar was basic, designed for working men who came in in their boots, but the walls were covered with photographs of local boats, the sea sweeping over their bows or engulfing them altogether, white spume flying, seagulls in their wake.

Rose knew many of the customers, as did Jack, who had been to school with some of them, and they were both at ease amongst these men. Their lives were dangerous but their living depended on the sea. They were loud, boisterous and often crude but this was one of their pubs and if others didn't like it they could leave. To the uninitiated the events which took place in the local bars would seem bizarre but Rose knew she would never be happy anywhere else.

They stayed for two drinks then Jack offered to walk her home. He noticed there was more colour in her solemn face. 'I've got next Wednesday off, fancy going out somewhere for the day?' He sometimes got the impression that she was about to say she didn't want to see him any more but she said yes, if a little distractedly, and he said he would pick her up at ten.

At her kitchen door he hesitated. Rose's head was bowed as she unlocked it. 'Thanks, Jack. 'Bye.'

'Yeah. See you.'

Rose closed the door and leant against it. 'Oh, Dorothy,' she whispered as she tried to stem the tears. Life seemed such a mess at times. Barry and Jack, both demanding her attention, Martin, left basically on his own, and Dorothy dead. 'Oh God.' She had not rung Barbara back and she was supposed to be going out with Laura that afternoon. At least she could sort one day out. Picking up the phone she chatted briefly to Barbara saying she was all right and that she would love to come to the party. How callous it sounded but Rose knew she had to start living properly, she had to start making things happen. Barbara sensed her need to be alone and did not keep her talking.

'Laura? It's me. Look, do you mind if we don't go today? I'm really not up to it.'

'Of course not. Want me to come over instead?'

They had planned to go to a car boot sale which was one of Laura's current crazes, then to a film in Truro.

'I, uh . . .'

'Rose, I'm coming anyway. I won't stay long, I just want to see for myself how you are.' Laura hung up. From the tone of her friend's voice she feared she might be slipping into a similar depression to the one she had suffered after David's death.

Although it wasn't far, Laura took the car, parking it untidily in the drive.

'What's it all about?' she demanded as soon as she arrived, dressed in ubiquitous leggings over which she wore a long silky shirt. Her hair was curling wildly around her shoulders. 'It's not just Dorothy, is it?'

Rose shook her head. 'No. It's everything.'

'Then sit down and tell Auntie Laura all about it.'

Rose did so, pouring out her fears that someone had murdered Dorothy and that Martin, who was confused, would get the blame and Gwen and Peter inherit everything. 'Jobber phoned me this morning. He's keeping an eye on Martin. I meant to go over myself but he doesn't know me that well.'

'Well, you can trust Jobber to see he's all right.'

'I know.'

'And?'

'Oh, Laura, it's Jack.'

'Yes. And dear devoted Barry, no doubt.'

Rose smiled weakly. 'How well you know me.'

'Just tell 'em both to bugger off. You're usually quite good at that sort of thing.'

And although Laura had promised not to stay long it was over two hours before she left and Rose was decidedly more cheerful.

It had been a dreadful weekend for Gwen and Peter Pengelly. Peter had arrived home on Friday to find his wife white-faced and almost incoherent. 'I'm sorry,' she kept repeating although he didn't know why. She had never liked his mother. 'I didn't want to contact you on the train – I mean, there was nothing you could do until you got home.'

He understood that. He'd have had to stay on the train anyway, even if they found another conductor to join it.

'Do the children know?'

'No, I thought it'd be better coming from you. They're next door. I didn't want them to overhear.' Gwen wondered how they would react to their first encounter with death although they had not known their grandmother very well. She had given no thought to Martin or to Dorothy's pets, her only concern was for Peter and how this would affect them all. Herself especially. Especially, she thought, after what she'd done.

Nothing mattered to her but her own family. From the time her own mother had died and left her and her brother in the care of a brutal, drunken father she had vowed that when she got married things would be very different. Peter, she adored, and she had made a career out of caring for the children and maintaining the solidarity of her family. Nothing was going to get in the way of that or stop her achieving her ambitions of a better life for all of them.

Only one thing nagged at her conscience. Peter was unaware of the visit she had made and it had to remain that way. Surely out there no one would have seen her car? But it was too late now to alter things, what had happened had happened and it just meant the money came to them sooner. I'm strong, she thought, strong enough for all of us. I must keep telling myself I didn't kill her and everything will be all right.

There had been no easy way to tell him. She had told the police she would do it herself, that he would want to hear it from her.

Peter's eyes were still wide with shock, he hadn't taken it in at first. 'When? When did she die?'

'They think it was some time last night.'

He shook his head in disbelief. 'No, not Mum, she can't be. It's a mistake. Mum was fitter than most women half her age.' He sank into a kitchen chair.

'It's true. They think it was probably her heart.' Gwen reached over and touched his hand.

'Don't.' He jerked it away as if she'd struck him. 'Don't. Just leave me alone.'

Startled, she drew back. Peter had never spoken to her in such a way.

'Oh God,' he muttered as he staggered to his feet. 'Oh, God, what have we done?' All the guilt rose up. 'We never went to see her, she hardly knew her grandchildren.'

No, Peter, what have I done? Gwen thought, ignoring his outburst. Visiting her more often wouldn't have prevented what had occurred on Thursday. 'Peter, wait.' Gwen watched in horror as he left the house, slamming the door behind him. It was the first time he had rebuffed her and it hurt all the more because her tactility had not been sexual. Suddenly the future was uncertain. This was a time she should be sharing with her husband but it seemed he did not need her.

'Is anything the matter?' Louise Hinkston whispered to her husband as she served the cheese course after dinner. They had guests again. Louise was very fond of entertaining and Bradley could usually be relied upon to ensure they were entertained. He had a fund of amusing anecdotes but he had been quiet throughout the meal.

He winked at her but did not reply. At the time, perhaps because of the influence of his surroundings, the oddly captivating atmosphere of a county where anything seemed, and often was, possible, he had not given much thought to the requests made of him. Only when he was back in familiar territory did he start to feel concerned. Bradley was not a man to worry unduly, his philosophy was that problems were simply there to be solved. Monday would be time enough to sort it out. And sorted out it must be. He was still unsure what Mrs Pengelly's motives had been and he could not afford to damage his reputation. What had happened could not be undone. He hadn't wanted to hear all the details but she did not spare him. If they find out, if they find out, he kept thinking.

'Bradley?' Louise was talking to him with her eyes, she was good at that. The message was, we have guests. Feeling more than one pair of inquisitive eyes upon him he forced himself to grin and began to charm his dinner guests.

Louise relaxed visibly and got up to bring in the coffee and brandy.

On Sunday he and Louise had lunch with their son and his wife who had just produced her second baby. It did not seem appropriate to closet himself in their library and make long-distance telephone calls when he was expected to make a fuss of the new child, but there were certain things he needed to verify. In the long run a weekday was better, he decided as Louise unobtrusively squeezed his arm. The bundled-up baby was passed to him. He smiled fondly at his grandson, wishing he had listened more carefully to what Mrs Pengelly had muttered as she had unwrapped newspaper from around a porcelain figurine. And how had a woman like that come to possess so many valuable items? The baby started to cry. Temporarily Bradley was distracted.

DI Jack Pearce decided to speak to each member of the Pengelly family. Just a casual chat, a few simple questions as to why Mrs Pengelly might have taken her own life. Although he usually trusted Rose's sixth sense, it seemed more likely that Dorothy had decided to end her life before she could no longer manage on her own. Rose had said her eyesight was failing. But she wasn't ill, Jack reminded himself. The pathologist had been surprised at how fit she had been. Martin was a strange boy and he drank. No, if alcohol had made him violent he'd have hit her or strangled her – and, according to Rose, he loved his mother. Peter, then. Had he got tired of waiting for his inheritance? There were few other people in Dorothy's life but he would have a quiet word with each. He was risking his neck. There was no evidence of any description, no suspicious circumstances at all, the verdict at the inquest would be suicide or death by misadventure if the old lady had swallowed more pills than she had intended. The latter seemed the most probable theory. Then where did she get the stuff?

He made himself concentrate on more pressing matters with the knowledge that he would have a whole day with Rose on Wednesday.

When Rose woke on Monday morning she felt as if a weight had been lifted from her. Since David's death she still had occasional bouts of depression but each time she seemed to recover more quickly. Energy flowed through her and she felt able to face the world and everyone in it. First there was work to be done. The proofs of photographs she had taken of a silver wedding anniversary were ready for the clients. She had put them in an album, a sales trick she had learnt because people tended to order more that way. Over coffee she worked out some figures. The album could be delivered on the way over to see Martin. She ought to have questioned him further about the men and how he thought he had killed his mother. Smiling because she knew what was happening, that she was, as Barry would say, about to poke her nose into other people's business, Rose left the house, swearing mildly as it began to drizzle. Ten minutes earlier there had been no sign of a cloud but already a sea fret was swirling around the base of the Mount leaving only the highest point visible. The sea had turned a steely grey and a heavy swell pushed it shorewards. She went back inside for the jacket which hung inside the pantry door. Once the small whitewashed room had been just that, now it housed the washing-machine and boxes of David's engineering textbooks which she could not bring herself to part with.

Grease streaked the windscreen as she drove away. Rose pressed the washer switch and cursed further as foam replaced the diesel smears. She had put too much washing-up liquid in the water.

Along the Promenade spray hit the car as the first waves of the high tide flung it up over the railing along with slimy bits of seaweed and a shower of small stones. It was early in the year for such weather but it would be far worse in February when gale force winds and torrential rain would cause the fishing-boats to lie idle far too long for the liking of their owners and their crews.

Stopping at a neat bungalow on the outskirts of Penzance, Rose hurried to the door and handed over the boxed package which contained the proofs. 'I'll let you know which ones I want within a couple of days,' Mrs Harvey told her. Rose refused the offer of a cup of coffee and returned to the car. The rain was coming down heavily and splashed against the back of her bare legs. Droplets of water ran down her face as she turned the ignition key, praying the engine would jump into life immediately. It did.

Leaving Penzance behind her she tried not to think of the scene which had awaited her on her last visit to Dorothy.

The sea fret had rolled inland and hung depressingly over the countryside and shrouded the house. Two stunted trees shed a deluge of water on to her as a gust of wind hit them. With a shudder Rose reached for the door handle.

It didn't turn. Martin had locked the door. She suspected Jobber had told him to do so. Rose let herself in. To her surprise everything was just as it had been when she had found Dorothy and Martin in the kitchen.

The cats were nowhere in sight but they had the freedom of the flap on the back door. Star was in her usual place, in her basket, and took no notice of her entry. Even George seemed to have lost some of his vitality: he did not growl at her or pretend to nip her ankles as she nervously crossed the kitchen expecting him to change his mind and remember to protect his territory. There was no sign of Martin but there was food in the animals' bowls and water in dishes. Feeling like the intruder she was, Rose checked the cupboards. There was a good supply of tins for both cats and dogs and an unopened sack of biscuits.

Feeling disorientated in Dorothy's empty kitchen she sat down in the seat where she had last drunk tea with her friend. She wondered if the dogs had been out but was not certain they would respond to her in the way in which they once had to Dorothy when she called them back. She took a chance and left the door open because the room smelt stale. Breathing in the moist air perfumed with gorse and heather, she watched Star stagger out of her basket, sniff the air herself then, in her less than youthful manner, lope up the side of the hill. George followed, yapping excitedly.

Through the kitchen window she watched the rain hitting the flagstones of the small yard where Dorothy used to hang her washing. Beyond it was the towering hill which always cast the room in shadow. A figure was approaching. Rose breathed a sigh of relief. It was Martin. He stood straighter and had more colour and if she failed, he'd get the dogs back in.

'I saw you,' he said, pointing over his shoulder as he stood in the doorway. 'I saw from up there that the door was open. I didn't know it was you, though, I thought they might have come back.'

'Who might have, Martin?' Rose stood, her hands at her sides, waiting. He knew something, of that she was sure, but whether it was relevant was difficult to tell. Outwardly he seemed to have accepted Dorothy's death. It was a mistake to have invited him to her house; Martin's solitude was not an enforced situation, it was one which he preferred and which she now saw would enable him to come to terms with his grief in much the same way as she had done.

'The men I spoke to.'

'I still don't understand, Martin. You told me you spoke to some men in me pub. Are you saying they came here?' She was, for the first time, alone with him in that large house with no one else around. For some reason she was afraid to ask him again why he thought he had killed his mother.

He nodded dumbly and looked at his feet then raised his eyes to stare at Dorothy's empty armchair. 'I didn't see 'em, but I know they came.'

Rose frowned in bewilderment. She had no idea what he was talking about. His next words made her catch her breath.

'Will you come upstairs with me?'

Rose inhaled deeply, trying to steady herself. There was no one for miles around and Martin was twice her size. Without meaning to she glanced at his muscled forearms before realising she was behaving neurotically. Martin would not hurt anyone. 'What for?'

'To see if they've taken anything.'

'Of course,' she said with relief.

She followed him up the uncarpeted stairs, their footsteps echoing. There was a sharp angle halfway up where three steps were triangular-shaped as the stairwell changed direction. Rose was careful to keep to the wider bits. The upstairs corridor was quite light as it reached a level with the brow of the hill. Martin, it seemed, believed that someone had come to the house with the intention of robbing Dorothy, but if that was the case why hadn't the police followed it up and why had he told her he thought he had killed her? There was the additional problem that although the police would not be able to tell if anything had been taken it was not certain that Martin would know either.

Rose had only been on the upper floor once, on the occasion when Dorothy had shown her the painting. Presumably Martin wasn't expecting her to recall what had been there but had needed company to make this search.

He opened the door of what used to be his own bedroom and stared around vacantly. It was sparsely furnished but had a panoramic view over the landscape with a distant hint of the sea. He shook his head. 'Nothing gone,' he said, closing the door. The next room, slightly larger, had been Peter's when a child but had long since been turned into a storeroom. Boxes were piled high on and around the single bed. Most were sealed and covered with dust. Only one had been opened, the cardboard flaps upright and yellowed newspaper lying crumpled on the floor as if something had been removed. To Rose it looked as if nothing else had been touched for years. Martin closed this door too but did not speak.

Outside the third one he hesitated. This was where his mother had slept, where she had slept all her married life and where she had given birth to both of her sons. 'I never went in here,' he offered and Rose saw that she had been right. This had been his mother's sanctuary, her one place of privacy, and he did not want to invade it alone. It was Rose who opened the door.

It was by far the biggest room and had two windows which looked out over the rainwashed countryside. The top of a minestack could be seen lower in the valley and cars, like small insects, wound their way along the main road. Opposite the window was the wooden-framed bed with its patchwork quilt. The pillowslips were white and clean, as was the edge of the sheet which was folded back over the blankets. On the chest which also served as a bedside table was a fringed reading lamp and a pile of books, Dorothy's place in the top one marked with an old envelope. The unread novel saddened Rose and she had to look away.

There was a wardrobe, probably Edwardian, and a small table beneath the windows. Everything was neat, everything seemed just as it ought to be. The Stanhope Forbes hung in its rightful place and there were no lighter patches on the faded wallpaper to indicate other paintings had been removed. 'Everything looks all right to me, Martin. Can you see anything wrong?'

He shook his head and stroked the patchwork quilt. Like Rose he was able to smell Dorothy's presence. Martin, she thought, was confused about the conversation in the pub which may or may not have taken place. He might even have dreamt it. 'Come on, let's go back down.' It was affecting them both, being in her room.

Rose turned to leave, her artist's eye naturally settling again on the Stanhope Forbes. Then she froze. 'Martin,' she finally said as calmly as she was able, 'did your mother keep her special things somewhere safe?' His brow creased with non-comprehension. 'I mean her paintings, did she put them somewhere safe and hang copies on the wall?'

'No. Not 'er. She liked her bits where she could see 'un.'

Rose stepped slowly towards the painting. It was identical to the one she had seen before, even down to the frame. Only this one was a print; not a copy, she had only used the word so as not to confuse Martin further. Had Dorothy noticed? Despite her pretence to the contrary, her eyesight wasn't good. But had Dorothy had time to notice? Was she dead even before it was swapped? Martin may not have been mistaken in thinking that the men he had spoken to had come to the house. Now you'll take me seriously, Jack Pearce, she thought. 'She hasn't changed this painting?' Rose pointed towards it; she had to be sure.

'No. 'Tis the same one.'

To Martin it probably seemed so. She had to let Jack know. If Dorothy had decided to put the original away for safekeeping it was not her place to make a thorough search of the house. But the police would need to speak to Martin and that worried her. If he repeated his fears that he had killed his mother they would question him endlessly and he would probably say things he didn't mean. There were other items to be considered, ones which Rose had not been shown and which might also be missing. She guessed that more valuables were stored in the boxes in Peter's old room. And one of those boxes had been opened.

Retracing her steps she peered into the other rooms. Her expert eye told her that what was on the walls had not been tampered with. There were one or two local scenes from some of the lesser known painters. Strange, then, that only one had been replaced, and why bother unless it was meant to conceal a crime? She smiled at Martin. 'I'll make us some tea. Do you think I could use the telephone?'

'Course you can. 'Er won't mind.'

As she preceded Martin down the narrow staircase she asked what he intended doing about the animals. For the time being they gave him something to do, a reason for getting out of the caravan rather than dwelling upon his mother's death.

'Well, I can't leave 'em starve. Me an' George've never got on too well but I expect he'll treat me different when he knows it's me what's going to feed him. I can't have them at the van, though, there's no room.'

Rose let it go. The house would be sold, or Gwen and Peter might live in it – either way, at some point a decision about the animals would have to be made. 'Martin, I've still got the keys. Do you want them back?'

He frowned with concentration. 'No, you keep 'em. I don't want Gwen out here.'

'All right, if you're sure.' She made tea and took out the mugs, pint pots that both Dorothy and her husband had favoured. 'What you told me,' she began, 'about those men. We're going to have to tell the police.'

'They'll lock us up, they buggers.'

Rose sipped her tea. By us he meant himself, and he might be right. 'Martin, you don't have to answer me but did your

85

mother . . . well, was she short of money?' It had only just occurred to her that Dorothy might have sold the painting and replaced it with the print by way of consolation.

'No, 'er always said she'd got more than she could possibly need.'

'All right, but we do have to let them know. If they need to ask you any questions I'll stay with you, all right?'

'I s'pose so. Ma said you was a sensible woman.'

Rose bent her head to hide an amused smile then stood and reached for the old-fashioned telephone. Jack wasn't at Camborne nor was he at home. She could have informed someone else but it did not seem appropriate and they might not have any idea what she was talking about. It could wait an hour. Martin's relief was obvious.

Rose looked around the kitchen and found a scrap of paper upon which she wrote her telephone number. 'Ring me any time you like. If there's anything at all you want, just let me know. Oh, if I'm out I've got an answering machine. All you have to do . . .' Seeing me hurt expression on Martin's face, Rose stopped.

'It's all right, Mrs Trevelyan, I aren't stupid. Your phone number's in the book and I know how to leave a message.'

Rose felt herself blushing under his scrutiny. How patronising she must have sounded. She would not compound her mistake by offering an apology. 'That's fine then,' she said briskly. 'Oh, and Martin, will you let me know about the funeral? I'd very much like to be there.'

'She'd want you to be and no mistake. She said you was 'er friend.'

'And she was mine.' Rose looked away, afraid she might

cry. 'Don't forget, if you need anything, let me know.'

'I suppose Peter'll see to the arrangements an' that. He never trusts me to do anything.'

'Yes, I expect he will. Shall we call the dogs in, it's getting late?'

Martin stepped out of the back door into the rain and gave a long, low whistle which brought the dogs, one bounding a little painfully, the other scurrying, but both saturated, to the back door. He held them away whilst they shook themselves. Star went straight to her basket, George stared balefully at Dorothy's chair then, reluctantly, leapt into it. He looked brighter now but Rose hoped not too bright to recall he was supposed to growl at visitors. She said goodbye to Martin and left him to lock up.

It was now impossible to sketch even under the protection of waterproofs and her golfing umbrella. The best of the light of a miserable day had already gone and the rain was falling in sheets, obscuring everything beyond a few yards' distance. Rose drove home slowly, peering through the windscreen as the wipers did their best to clear the spray the traffic in front was throwing up. It was an afternoon to be spent in the attic where she would start on the watercolouring of some previous work. The northern light would be of no use today but the lamps which she had had fitted and which gave off the next best thing to daylight would have to suffice.

Sodden and wet-footed, Rose kicked off her shoes inside the kitchen door and hung her jacket on its hook in the pantry where it dripped over the floor. The fluorescent light buzzed as she flicked the switch and its brightness illuminated the room. Water from the gutters gurgled down the drainpipe, rain lashed against the window and the sea rolled relentlessly towards the land. She seemed to be in a liquid world with wetness everywhere.

Leaving the kettle to boil she went up to shower, throwing her clothes into the wicker laundry basket. She would not be going out again so dressed only in underwear and a long towelling robe. Feeling rather like a schoolgirl playing truant she ignored the kettle which had already boiled and pulled a bottle of dry white wine from the fridge. Jack often made sarcastic remarks about her having more alcohol than food in store but, she thought, Jack could do the other thing. She poured a glassful and took a sip before carrying it upstairs where she succeeded in doing a couple of hours' work uninterrupted.

Three small paintings complete Rose had the satisfaction of knowing that they were better than she had anticipated. The sky was lighter now. Without her noticing the rain had eased considerably and the blackest of the clouds had rolled eastwards. 'Rain heading from the west,' she muttered. Someone elsewhere was in for it. She conscientiously cleaned her brushes then went down to her bedroom to study the view because there might be a rainbow.

Fingers of sunlight lit up the white windmills which produced electricity on the hills far across the bay. It was not often she could see them. The sea was now aquamarine in the foreground and deeper blue in the distance. You are procrastinating, she told herself, you know you really ought to tell someone about Dorothy's painting even if you do make a fool of yourself. Before ringing Jack's direct line at Camborne she poured another glass of wine to give her courage. There was no answer. She sighed. But at least temporarily it solved the problem. Half an hour later she tried again. 'It mightn't mean anything, Jack, but—'

'When you come out with things like that my nerves start jangling,' he interrupted.

She could hear the smile in his voice but there was no sudden desire to see him although she knew that she must. 'I think it might be better if we spoke face to face.'

'Is that a veiled invitation, Mrs Trevelyan?'

'It might be important,' she snapped, sorry he had misinterpreted her words.

'Put like that, I can hardly refuse. I won't get away until eight, is that too late?' His tone was mildly sarcastic.

'No.' Wearily she relented. 'You can share my supper if you want.'

'Is it something I like?'

'For goodness' sake, Jack, I—'

'Only teasing. See you later.' And with that he hung up.

Jack Pearce is no one's fool, she thought, and although Rose liked to keep him at arm's length, he was quite adept at the same game himself. She busied herself preparing the meal then remembered she wasn't dressed. She did not want Jack to get the wrong idea. Remedying the situation she put on tan tailored trousers, a cream shirt and a brown cord waistcoat. She loosened her hair to brush it. There were waves where the band had constricted it and the dampness had dried and shaped it. Rose turned her head in front of the mirror and decided it looked quite nice.

It was a quarter to nine before Jack's car pulled into the drive. She had poured him a glass of wine before he reached the kitchen door.

* * *

Fred Meecham sat at Marigold's bedside holding her hand. She had been in a coma when he arrived but he whispered softly to her. The nurse had said she might be able to hear him. The words he used were gentle and loving and he carried on talking even after he knew she could no longer hear him.

'Mr Meecham, come away now.'

'What are you going to do with her?'

'We're going to put on a clean nightdress,' the nurse explained tactfully. 'I'm really sorry, you were so close to your sister, weren't you?' She touched his hand, knowing there was nothing he could say. 'Is there someone we can telephone to take you home?'

Fred shook his head. Home. The word was meaningless now. He shuffled out of the ward, turning back too late because the curtains had been redrawn around Marigold's bed. No! he wanted to scream, but he knew it was no use. Down in the car park he sat cocooned in the car watching the rain stream down the windscreen. It was as if with the final closing of Marigold's eyes his own had been opened. He saw himself for the hypocrite he was, his whole life a lie. Yes, he believed in and prayed to God but he had broken many of the commandments. He took no comfort in the fact that none of it had been for himself; it did not lessen the wrongness of the deeds. Had Dorothy been right all along? Now was not the time to think of Dorothy.

He drove home and sat in the flat with the lights off, his head in his hands. If he had been a drinking man he reckoned he would have got drunk. But he wasn't, it was one of the vices he did not have.

Later that evening when Fred went downstairs to answer

the summons of the bell at the side of the shop door he initially thought that it might be a customer in urgent need of something. Then he wondered if his thoughts had somehow transmitted themselves to the rest of the world. Why else should the police be standing on his doorstep? All that other business was years ago.

'What a great welcome. Cheers.' He took a sip of wine. He had been expecting Rose to behave coldly towards him. Pulling out a chair he sat down and leant back. Rose wondered what it was that made people more comfortable in her kitchen than anywhere else in the house. 'Now, are you going to tell me what it is that might or might not be important?' Quite relaxed, he crossed his legs.

Rose explained about the painting, adding the alternative possibilities she had worked out for herself.

'But the others are still hanging, you say?'

'Yes. And there're a couple that are worth a few bob.'

Jack was thoughtful. 'So why not take them all? Look, Rose, a thief isn't going to bother to swap a painting.'

'Why not? What if he knows Dorothy can't see too well, what then?'

'You have a point, but how would he have had access to her bedroom?'

'You're supposed to be the detective.'

'Yes, but you think like one. Answer me this one, then. If the drugs were not self-administered, how come she didn't notice them being forced down her throat or taste them in something or other?'

Rose shrugged expressively, causing her hair to fall

forward. Jack reached out to push it back, touching her face as he did so. Rose's head jerked up, startling Jack.

'What is it?'

'Alcohol.'

'Alcohol?'

'You said the police surgeon noticed the smell, I did too. Dorothy didn't drink. Well, not really. A glass of sherry on special occasions. If someone gave her, say, whisky, she wouldn't have noticed.' Her face was animated. Whatever Jack Pearce decided, she was going to discover the truth. 'Perhaps whoever it was didn't mean to kill her, just knock her out for a while. Perhaps they didn't realise she wasn't used to drink or medication of any sort.'

Jack was only half listening. What had happened to the paracetamol bottle? If it had contained the means of Dorothy's death there might be fingerprints. 'Rose, as I said, I'd already decided to ask a few questions. I think I ought to start tonight. But tell me one thing, you're certain that what you saw the first time was an original?'

'Yes.'

Then it was worth a considerable sum and, with the way things were in the county at the moment, enough to consider murdering for. Fishing-boats were being decommissioned whilst foreign ships trawled British waters and the Government as well as the EU thumbed its nose, South Crofty, the last working tin mine, was on the verge of shutting down unless something truly drastic happened and the towns and villages that had relied upon both industries were fast losing their identity as the once proud miners and fishermen became no more than statistics in the unemployment figures. Jack ground his teeth. And the beef crisis was causing farmers to tear their hair out. Their three main industries were being wiped out and Cornwall, his birthright, was being sanitised for the sake of the emmets who littered the place with their fast food containers and ignored the signs telling them not to feed the gulls and who preferred the tourist attractions and visitor centres to the unspeakable beauty all around them. He was angry, with himself as well as the world, because he was powerless to change the way things were going, angry also with the people who brought to Cornwall or expected to find here all that they had come to escape. One bloody great theme park, that's what we'll be, he thought. Youngsters were moving away because the average wage would have been laughed at elsewhere. Yes, he decided, an original Stanhope Forbes was definitely worth killing for.

'Jack?'

'I'm sorry, Rose, I was thinking.' The scowl left his face because of the concern showing in hers. 'Well, not thinking exactly, more like conducting a mental diatribe against the human race.'

'Me included?'

'No, Rose, never you. I'll have to go. I'm sorry. I hope you didn't go to too much trouble with the meal. What was it anyway?'

'Monkfish with fennel.'

He groaned. 'Just my luck. I'll make it up to you.'

'No need.' Just get to the bottom of this, Jack, she thought as she bolted the kitchen door behind him.

'Shall I come back later?' he called through the partly open window.

Rose looked down. 'No, not tonight.'

She might as well eat, and eat a proper meal. As she slid the monk into the pan she tried to see if she could be wrong, if there had been anything different about Dorothy on her last few visits. There hadn't, not unless she counted that business with the envelope. 'Oh, no!' The fish slice clattered to the floor. All that fussing around with the envelope – had that been a pantomime she was meant to remember? The last time she had been to see her, Dorothy had slipped something into an A5 envelope, written ostentatiously on the front, sealed it and tossed it into a kitchen drawer in a rather dramatic manner. Surely it wasn't a suicide note? There's only one way to find out, she decided. But it was too late that night.

Fred Meecham's sister, Marigold, outlived Dorothy Pengelly by only a couple of days. Naturally it was Doreen Clarke who rang Rose the following morning to tell her. 'I know you never met her, but you know Fred and I thought you might want to write a note or something. The shop's shut, he's put a sign on the door. It'll be a double blow for him. First Dorothy, now this. It's awful, isn't it, both of them going in a week?'

Going. Typical Doreen, Rose thought. If there was a euphemism available Doreen would use it. Rose had met Fred Meecham on several occasions when he had stopped at Dorothy's place to deliver a case of dog food or a box of heavy groceries, and once or twice she had been into his shop. With her painter's eye, in the way she did with all interesting faces, Rose had committed the details of his to her mind. He had a shock of red hair which seemed to have a life of its own. With his washed-out blue irises and pallid complexion he was far from attractive but his lean body and sensual mouth made him seem so. His Cornish accent was not pronounced and bespoke his Truro origins. Dorothy had told Rose about the sister, Marigold, and had said she thought it was time that Fred faced up to the gravity of the situation. 'He won't allow himself to believe she's dying. And he should have more sense than to think money can solve everything,' she had said. 'It's going to hit him hard when it happens.' At that point Dorothy had clammed up, realising – too late – that it was another painful reminder for Rose.

'I'll be going to the funeral,' Doreen continued. 'I'm sure most of Fred's customers will be there. I wonder if he'll close the shop that day, too? Out of respect, like. Dear me, it's ages since I've been to one, do people still wear black? Doesn't seem right somehow, not for someone so young. She was only in her forties.'

'Wear whatever you feel comfortable in, Doreen,' Rose answered, allowing her chatter to drift over her head. Face to face she enjoyed her company but it was often difficult to end a telephone conversation. Rose finally replaced the receiver. Having met Fred on so few occasions she wondered if it was appropriate to send a message of condolence. On the other hand they had both been friends of Dorothy so there was a mutual, if tenuous bond. She got out a pen and some paper.

Twice during the course of the day Rose heard the telephone ringing but she did not bother to answer it – she rarely did if she was working. There were many jobs to catch up on and she wanted them all out of the way before she sat down and made some serious plans, which she intended doing that evening.

Later she carefully rewrote the note to Fred Meecham, realising as she did so what the many people who had written to her during her bereavement had gone through. Almost satisfied she put down her pen. The phone rang again. Unthinkingly she reached out a hand and picked up the receiver, resting it between her shoulder and her ear. 'Hello?' she said cheerfully.

'Keep out of it. Just keep out of it or you're dead.'

'But . . . ? Who are you?' But the line had been disconnected. Rose sat very still as she tried to work out if she had heard that voice before. She did not think so. And keep out of what? Dialling 1471 she learnt that the caller had withheld their number. She was not easily frightened but that evening she turned on the lights before they were strictly needed.

Fear turned to anger. She would not be intimidated by anyone, least of all an anonymous caller. Despite her intentions not to do as Jack had requested and speak to the Pengelly family, she changed her mind. Whoever had threatened her knew something which could only be connected with Dorothy's death. But why the threat? What had she done to induce it? Nothing, as far as she knew. Not yet.

CHAPTER SIX

The unexpectedness of his mother's death had shocked Peter Pengelly more than the event itself. When Gwen had told him, he had had to get out of the house. The overwhelming grief he felt was genuine, worsened by his sense of guilt. None of this hit him at first. Since then the police had been back, wanting to know if Dorothy had complained of feeling ill or depressed or if she had expressed any financial worries or any worries whatsoever. Shamefully Peter had admitted that they did not see much of his mother.

For the first time in his life he viewed his childhood days objectively. He had never been as close to his mother as Martin and, since the day he had started school, he had steadily grown away from her. He wondered if this was because Martin had remained at home for another two years and therefore he was jealous or if he had always suspected his brother was the favourite.

As a child and a young man Peter had found his mother odd, even eccentric, although he wasn't sure why. She was a good deal older than most of the mothers who collected their children from school, some no more than girls themselves who had married at sixteen or seventeen. Peter could have borne the age discrepancy if Dorothy had not gone out of her way to disregard generally held opinions and to distance herself from his friends' mothers who huddled in groups outside the school gates.

On the death of his father her grief had seemed disproportionate. His limited experience of such things told him that people quietly wiped away the tears and suffered stoically until a normal life could be resumed. Not so his mother. She had sobbed and screamed and shouted, waving her fists in the air and railing against God. Now and then she had thrown things, but never at her sons. With them she had been loving and understanding. In the privacy of their home Peter was able to shut out these scenes by going to his room. To drown out the sounds he would play his transistor radio loudly and pretend it wasn't happening. He did not know how to cope with such an excess of pain.

Martin had either been impervious to it or had instinctively known how to deal with it. He would remain at his mother's side, quietly playing with his toys or struggling with homework he could not understand. When Dorothy was calmer he would climb on to her knee and stroke her face.

It became embarrassing for Peter at school. Dorothy had inherited their father's car and she had learnt how to drive it. Instead of coming in on the bus to meet them she would sit behind the wheel, parked some distance away safely out of reach of any words of sympathy that might have been offered. This alienated her from the other mothers further.

Then one day, as if some dramatic catalyst had occurred whilst they were all asleep, Peter came downstairs to find his mother cooking a proper breakfast and humming as she did so. Neither his father nor God were mentioned again and an old photograph of Arthur Pengelly, which Peter had not known existed, appeared on Dorothy's bedside table, framed in wood.

And now she was gone and he could understand what she must have felt but it was too late to tell her so. Bitterly he wished he had spent more time with her, told her that he loved her, because now he realised that he did. All those years she had lived up at the house, alone after Martin left, and he had no idea what went on in her head or if she thought of him at all.

He had used Gwen and the children as an excuse, as a reason for being too busy to visit. He loved them, too, of course. Gwen could be overpowering at times and usually got her own way. She also had a far greater need for sex than he did, which wore him out Her insecurity in such matters was exhausting. He tried not to disappoint her but it was difficult at times, and he knew she bought the underwear because she thought it would please him. He did not have the heart to say it didn't matter, that he did not expect her to be like a film star all the time. He would have liked to come home one day and find her in a pair of jeans, her hair tousled, like other young mothers. He suspected Gwen was compensating for what she considered to be his own mother's sloppy ways, trying to prove what a good wife she was by comparison. She had nothing to fear, there was no competition.

He had walked miles on that Friday evening, tiring

himself physically but unable to still his thoughts. Very quietly he had let himself into the almost silent house. The children were in bed but a few faint sounds came from the kitchen. He had sat in his armchair in the small lounge and leant back against the cushions. Without warning his throat began to ache and hot tears filled his eyes. He had not cried for years and he wondered if his own tears were a substitute for the ones neither his wife nor his children had shed. It was a sad reflection on them all that they had hardly known their grandmother.

Gwen had opened the door, a dishcloth in her hand. 'I thought I heard you come in,' she said gently. 'I've kept our meal hot.' She hesitated in the doorway. Peter's shoulders were bowed and she did not know how to go about comforting him because she was afraid of another rebuffal. She was glad the children could not see him like this. 'Peter?' She advanced slowly.

Reaching out blindly he had pulled her to him, sobbing wetly into the thin cotton of her dress. Without warning his grip tightened and Gwen fell on top of him. Before she could protest he had tugged at her buttons and pulled the dress open.

'Peter,' she had protested, but it was useless, he had pinned her down and was inside her, moving frantically as if the act could expurgate all the guilt and sorrow he felt. Gwen was too stunned to struggle. It had never been like that before.

When it was over Peter sat up and ran a hand through his hair without looking at her. 'It's what you've always wanted, isn't it? Just like you've always wanted my mother dead.' He turned to see her face, her mouth open in horror. Getting to his feet he adjusted his clothes and left the house again with no idea where he was going.

Tireder still, he had walked fast and without thought, trying to numb all emotions. Heedless of the dewlike moisture which clung to his clothes he headed towards the soft white sand of the Towans and walked down to the water's edge where it was damp beneath his feet and the soles of his shoes left impressions in the sand. It seemed as if he might walk straight into the sea.

The rhythmic slap of the shallow waves against the beach had soothed him. The tide was receding and through the still night air the calls of oystercatchers feeding on the estuary carried over the water. Two gulls huddled nearby, facing the breeze, shifting slightly as he approached.

Not once had he wished his mother harm. Yet look what he had just done to Gwen, proving he was capable of violence. His face reddened with shame. 'Goddammit!' he shouted. 'I should have revelled in my mother's differences.' All he had done was to pretend they had not existed.

It was very late by then and Gwen would be worried. Peering at the luminous dial of his watch he saw it was after midnight. He had to face her at some point so he began the long walk home, his footsteps dragging through the dunes. Below him the harbour lights winked. The drizzle had eased but in the distance a fine mist hung beneath the lights of the bypass. By the time he got home he felt a tiny surge of optimism. It was not too late to become a decent human being.

Gwen had been too shocked to cry or to question Peter's behaviour, which was beyond her comprehension. As soon as he had left she went upstairs to shower, glad that both children were asleep. Feeling dirty and defiled she let the hot water run over her body for fifteen minutes yet she had to admit that Peter was right in a way. She was sexually demanding but she had been brought up to believe that that was what men wanted, that if you were not available and willing they would find someone who was. Her father, when he had hit her, used to say that it was for her own good, that it was because he loved her. Gwen had grown up requiring endless proof that she was loved and desirable.

There would be no repeat performance that night. Her hair damp and wearing only an old T-shirt of Peter's, she had gone back downstairs to wait. She was anxiously chewing the skin around her nails when he returned. Whatever happened the police must not find out about that evening. If they thought that Peter was a violent man what else might they think? Gwen decided she would never mention it.

When Peter came into the kitchen she felt as though she had been holding her breath. He looked her up and down and took in the unmade-up face, the bare feet and the tatty T-shirt. She had not blow-dried her hair and it lay flat against her skull. Never before had she looked so young and so vulnerable. 'Oh, Gwen,' he said, reaching for her and pulling him to her. 'I don't know what to say.'

'Let's forget it, shall we? I'll make us some tea.'

Peter nodded. 'That'd be nice.'

Gwen pulled away from him and in a businesslike way got out the cups and saucers. The temptation to tell him what she had done had completely disappeared.

Two days later things were back to normal until the

police had returned with their questions. Peter, grey and old-looking, had only shaken his head when they mentioned the word suicide. Gwen had become hysterical and if one of the detectives hadn't calmed her down he was sure he would have slapped her. Peter's guilt increased with the knowledge that his mother had been unhappy enough to take her own life. He was unable to see in which direction the questions were heading.

Rose stretched then sat up in bed, brushing the hair out of her eyes as she squinted at the alarm clock. Seven thirty-five. She had had a good night's sleep after all. Sliding back down under the duvet she felt warm and comfortable, until she remembered the telephone call and what she had determined to do.

She slipped out of bed and went downstairs to make tea. The sun slanted in through the sitting-room window where the curtains were never drawn. Rose could not bear to shut out that view. As the kettle boiled she scanned the sky with its promise of a fine day, although she knew how often those promises were not fulfilled. The warning horn of a beamer boomed out as it negotiated the gap between the two piers and left the harbour. Out in the bay it gathered speed, bowing and dipping, spray flying along its sides although the sea was cellophane smooth from where she stood.

The kitchen was cool. Only when the sun was setting did the golden rays reach the side window. Rose poured boiling water on to the tea leaves in the pot and lit the grill to make toast. She had never possessed a toaster and guessed that she and David must have been the only couple not to have been given one as a wedding present. Sadly she got out the last jar of orange marmalade, one of a batch which Dorothy had made and given to her.

Opening the door to enjoy the weather Rose realised how few such days were left before the storms of winter set in for real. After the rain the grass was verdant once more. She stood and watched a blackbird who, head on one side, was also watching her as he finished his business of stamping on her unkempt lawn to bring the worms to the surface. She smiled. He must have been hungry for her presence did not deter him. Finally he succeeded in his task. Watching him eat reminded her that Barry Rowe was cooking her a meal that evening. It was quite a while since she had been to his flat.

Rose took her breakfast upstairs and ate it in bed, having drawn back the curtains and opened the window fully in order to watch the beamer's progress. It was already passing in front of the Mount. She cursed when the phone rang as she had to go downstairs to answer it. She kept meaning to get an extension for the bedroom.

'Rose, it's Jack. I've got to cancel, I'm afraid. There's someone off sick and they want me to go in. I'll make it up to you, I promise.'

'It's okay. Really.' Wednesday. She had completely forgotten they were supposed to be spending the day together. You don't love him, girl, Rose told herself, you've got to do something about him. Yet she had remembered her date with Barry. Barry she did love, but as a friend, one she would not let down if she could possibly help it.

'Sure?'

'Positive.'

'Yes . . .' Jack paused, unsure what to say. 'Well, goodbye then.'

Rose knew she had not sounded disappointed. She shrugged. There was no point in encouraging him.

She ran a bath and whilst it was filling opened the cabinet to get out a new bar of soap. On the shelf were the disposable razors she had bought for Jack because she did not want to see his own where David's had once lain. Or so she had thought. Now she realised that was not the sole reason, it was also because Jack's own razor in her bathroom would have smacked of a permanence she did not want. Is that how I see Jack, too? she thought. As disposable?

She bathed quickly and tidied the kitchen, throwing more washing into the machine in case the weather held. 'He's got a nerve,' she said aloud, unfairly blaming him when she knew she could have called a halt to the relationship at any time. And then to suggest she had a word with the Pengellys on the feeble pretext that she was offering condolences – who did he think she was? He had said that Peter and Gwen had already been questioned but he would be interested in her opinion. She would do it but on her own terms, for herself but, more importantly, for Dorothy. Then she would have to decide whether or not to mention any of it to Barry whose reaction she could predict. The threatening telephone call was still on her mind. Only Jack and Barry were aware of her suspicions. And Martin. She stifled the thought. Barry would not have discussed them with anyone so how could anyone know what was on her mind? Laura? No, not Laura and not Doreen Clarke either. Besides, she was sure it was a man's voice. It didn't make sense, it was as if someone was already outguessing her. Foolish, maybe, to ignore the threat but her stubbornness dictated that she would try harder to find out why Dorothy had died.

One of the wild flowers listed by Barry grew close to the Hayle estuary. Rose took this as a sign. She would call upon the Pengellys because she had reason to be in the area. Jack had told her that Peter worked shifts but had taken some compassionate leave and was almost certain to be at home. She had met him only once; Gwen she had never met.

Throughout the short drive she tried to plan what she would say but her mind kept returning to the phone call. It was silly not to have mentioned it to Jack. If there was another one she would do so.

The house was exactly as Dorothy had portrayed it on an occasion when she had tried to describe her daughter-in-law. 'Typical Gwen,' she had said. 'Neatness means more to 'er than anything.' It was one in a terrace which stepped down towards the estuary. The lower halves of the buildings were brick, the tops pebble-dashed and painted white. Each had a small shed to the side of the front door with its entrance at right angles to the house. There were spotless net curtains at the windows. In front was a small patch of grass. Tiny wooden fences divided the gardens.

Rose rang the bell. She knew from Dorothy that Gwen did not go out to work so it was likely that both Pengellys would be in. 'Mrs Pengelly?' Rose smiled warmly then realised it was a mistake. The woman in front of her was slender and beautiful in a waif-like way but her features showed signs of misery. She had not expected this reaction, not after what Dorothy had led her to believe. But Rose did not know about the events which had shaken Gwen to the core. Sizing her up quickly, Rose took in the expensive haircut, the straight blue skirt, soft blouse and high-heeled shoes. It seemed an incongruous outfit for a housewife and mother on a weekday, one who was recently bereaved. 'I'm Rose Trevelyan. Dorothy may have mentioned me.'

'Yes. Yes, I believe she did. You paint or something, don't you? Won't you come in?'

Rose nodded. This was a far cry from Doreen Clarke's extravagant praise of the way in which she earned her living. Doreen had obliquely let it be known that she did not like Gwen Pengelly but Rose would not let her opinion cloud her own judgement.

'Would you like some coffee?'

'If you're not too busy. I only came to say how sorry I was. Dorothy was a good friend to me.'

Gwen seemed surprised to hear this. 'I see.' She plugged in a percolator. 'Please sit down. Excuse me, I must put these in.' Gwen picked up a pile of children's clothes and bundled them into the washing-machine.

It was such an ordinary, everyday domestic task yet Rose would have been less surprised if she had said she was about to leave for a modelling engagement. In her faded denim skirt, a pink and yellow checked shirt, frayed rope espadrilles and her soft hair already escaping from the wooden clasp at the nape of her neck, Rose felt a complete mess beside her. One day she really would do something about her wardrobe. The sound of running water filled the sunlit room as the machine filled then began its cycle.

Gwen stood up and looked at her hands as if she was unsure what to do with them. 'We were going to see her on Sunday. Dorothy.'

'I'm sorry. It must have been a dreadful shock for you.'

'It was.'

'Do you know when the funeral will be held?'

'It'll be at Truro Crematorium but we haven't got a date yet. We can't do anything until after the inquest on Friday. If you leave me your phone number I'll let you know.'

'Thank you.' Rose rummaged in her shoulder bag for one of her business cards.

Gwen took it and read it slowly. 'Look, I apologise. I didn't mean to sound offhand. It hasn't been easy lately.' She paused. It would have been pleasant to confide in another woman but she did not know Rose Trevelyan. 'At least Dorothy had a reasonably long life. We must be grateful for that. Oh, Peter, I thought you'd gone out.'

Neither of them had heard the door leading to the hall open. There had been no other sounds in the house and she, too, had imagined Peter was out. It was him she had come to see but she had the feeling that Gwen had been about to confide in her. She watched them both: there was tension between them.

Standing in the doorway, looking unsure of himself, Peter's hand was still on the handle. 'I heard the bell. I came down to see if it was the police again. It's Mrs Trevelyan, isn't it?' Rose nodded. 'I thought I remembered you.' Dressed far more casually than his wife, in jeans and a sweatshirt, Peter had not yet shaved. His hair showed the first signs of thinning in small indentations at each temple.

'I came to say how sorry I am about your mother.'

'We meant to telephone. We said we would, didn't we, Gwen? The police told us you did what you could to help. Martin wouldn't have been capable of coping on his own. It was a good job you were passing. Thank you.'

Rose saw that Peter was right. Martin was not stupid but, left to his own devices, he might have sat there, rocking Dorothy, for hours. 'Thank you.' Gwen had placed three cups of coffee on the table.

'I'm just glad the children are back at school. It's better for them. If this had happened during the summer holidays . . .' The sentence trailed off and Gwen shrugged.

'God, nothing seems to make sense,' Peter said, ignoring his wife's comments. 'First they lead us to believe she had a heart attack, then they tell us it's suicide, but when that inspector bloke turned up on Monday night we didn't know what he was getting at.'

So Jack had come here after leaving her place. He had not mentioned that when he rang earlier. And she hadn't mentioned the threatening call. If they were back to playing those games Rose was determined to win.

'Who could possibly wish her harm? She was just an old lady. I mean, no one went out there, did they?' Peter had slumped into a chair.

Rose knew that Dorothy had more friends than he realised. He was, she saw, genuinely upset whereas Gwen almost shrugged it off. Something different was troubling her; she seemed to be under a lot of strain. Women use drugs and poison far more than men. The thought flashed through her mind. Don't be so stupid, she told herself.

'It must have been awful for you, walking in on it.' Gwen decided it was time she made a contribution.

'It wasn't very pleasant How's Martin?' Rose could have predicted the answer.

'Martin?' Gwen glanced briefly at her husband.

'He prefers to be up at the caravan,' Peter put in quickly, ashamed that he had only tried once to find him despite his intention to behave decently. But Martin had not contacted them either. 'I expect you know that,' he continued with a ready excuse. 'I heard that he went home with you but didn't want to stay.'

'He doesn't feel things the way most people do.' This was from Gwen. Rose thought it was the strangest comment she had heard in a long time. Gwen sighed. 'There's such an awful lot to do and we can't start until the police give us the go-ahead. We can't even put the house on the market yet.'

Rose raised an eyebrow in surprise. Gwen was taking a lot upon herself unless she knew for certain that it had been left to her. And poor Martin, it was as if he did not exist. It was not her place to bring it up but Jack, damn him, had encouraged her. Besides, she liked Dorothy's younger son and someone had to be on his side. 'Won't Martin have some say in the matter?'

Gwen made a sound which Rose could not interpret. 'Oh, he's just fine up in that van of his. He won't be interested in the house. Anyway, Dorothy told me she'd left a will and that she'd done the right thing by us. We've got a young family to bring up. After all, Martin's only got himself to think about.'

'Mm.' Rose was non-committal. Dorothy could be cryptic

at times and it was extremely doubtful that she would let Martin lose out financially. But perhaps she was wrong.

Peter had clammed up and seemed content to let his wife do all the talking. He blew on his coffee and avoided making eye contact with either of the women. Rose did not know how or whether she should bring up the subject of the Stanhope Forbes. To her surprise Gwen did it for her.

'She's got some lovely old pieces up there. And her paintings. There're some very good ones. We'll probably keep a couple, I expect, but the rest will have to be sold.'

Peter seemed unperturbed by the mercenary turn in the conversation. He might have been in a world of his own except for what he did next. He got up abruptly, almost knocking over his chair. 'It's my mother you're talking about,' he hissed at Gwen then left the room, banging the door behind him. Rose had listened carefully, trying to think how the voice on the telephone had sounded, but she couldn't be sure. Taking her cue she stood too. There was nothing to be learnt from Peter and whatever Gwen had been about to tell her earlier she would not find out now. 'Thank you for the coffee. If there's anything I can do, well, you've got my number.'

'Thanks. I won't forget to let you know the date of the funeral.' Gwen walked her to the door and closed it as soon as Rose had stepped outside. She had learnt little other than that Gwen was neurotic, and whether or not there was a will it was up to a solicitor to sort out. She could not see Martin switching that painting, but if Peter suspected he had been left nothing could he have done so? There would have been no problem in gaining access to the house, Dorothy would have let him in unquestioningly. Was that why Gwen was so anxious? Did she know something? Rose shook her head. Nothing seemed to make any sense. She got into the car and drove down the hill convinced that there was more to it than a missing painting. There were undercurrents in the Pengelly household which she could not define. And she had taken an instant dislike to Gwen which might interfere with her objectivity. She would sketch the damn flower then go and see Martin.

Bradley Hinkston told his wife that he would be away overnight again. She seemed not to be listening. Seated at the breakfast bar, both elbows resting on its surface, she held a magnifying mirror in one hand and a mascara wand in the other. Clad in cream leather trousers and a scarlet silk shirt Louise was preparing for a morning's shopping and lunch with a girlfriend. The breakfast dishes lay scattered around – they and the rest of the chores would be left for the woman who came in to see to them. 'Louise, did you hear me?'

'Sorry, darling.' She looked up and smiled. 'Can't talk when I'm doing my eyes. Just tonight, is it?'

'I think so. I'll let you know either way.'

'Good. I don't like it when you're not here.' Her actions seemed to belie her words because she immediately turned away and stretched her lips to apply lipstick.

Cursing mildly as the sleeve of his jacket brushed spilt tea on the work surface, Bradley reached down and picked up his briefcase. He could not really blame Louise. She ran her own beauty business, although nowadays she mostly left the manager in charge, and she had as little inclination towards housework as he had himself.

It was mild but overcast as he left the outskirts of Bristol behind him and, as the holiday brochures optimistically promised, the nearer he came to his destination the warmer it was and the brighter the sun shone. He knew from experience that this was not always the case. Twice before he had driven into heavy rain. Depressing the switch which activated the electronic windows he felt the breeze produced by the speed of the car cool his face. It was more subtle than the consistent air-conditioning. With luck he would get accommodation at the same place. It was clean and comfortable, the room was attractive and the food was plentiful and good. Better still, the landlord did not hurry him upstairs once the bar was officially closed. Bradley had stayed in hotels which were of a lower standard. By himself he was quite happy with bed and breakfast. When Louise accompanied him she preferred more luxurious surroundings.

Dorothy Pengelly was an interesting woman and she had made him an interesting proposition but he hadn't trusted her to keep quiet about it. Initially it had crossed his mind that senility had taken a grip but, on reflection, he sensed that she was an extremely acute old lady and knew far more about what made people tick than he did himself and he was no fool.

The season may have been over but there was still plenty of traffic heading towards the south-west. A caravan swayed dangerously ahead of him and as soon as he had an opportunity he overtook it. The driver of the car towing it was travelling too fast. He tooted his horn and gestured towards the rear vehicle as he passed it but the driver ignored him.

First things first, he decided as he left the A30 at the Hayle junction. He pulled up in the car park of the pub where he had stayed before and went into the bar. Lunchtime customers were ordering food. Bradley was flattered to be remembered by the landlord.

'Same room if you like,' he was told. 'The missus'll show you up. Let her know if there aren't any towels. We weren't expecting much more trade.'

Bradley entered the low-ceilinged bedroom with its tiny *en suite* bathroom. There was a shower stall, a lavatory and a small hand basin. The plumbing was efficient and it was adequate for his needs. He hung up the spare clothes he had brought and placed his toilet bag on the glass shelf above the sink. After splashing his face with cold water he went down to the bar for a quick drink before going over to the Pengelly place. It was a risk returning, he knew that, especially if what he had learnt about the daughter-in-law was true. Gwen Pengelly was angling to get Dorothy into an old people's home in order to get her hands on her possessions. It was too late now for Gwen Pengelly to have her way; Dorothy had made other arrangements.

Marigold's funeral was not taking place until the following week. Fred had needed time to let everyone know and he felt it would have seemed like rushing her departure from the world if he took the first date which was offered. He could not contemplate how he would get through the intervening days. It was unbearable in the shop receiving the pitying glances and hearing the well-meaning words of his customers. 'She's no longer suffering,' was the most oft repeated. Fred wanted to shout at them, to say that she shouldn't have been made to suffer at all. It was even more unbearable upstairs in the flat with nothing but his own thoughts for company and Marigold's possessions all around him.

Out of a perverse desire to please, he had lined up the condolence cards he had received from his customers on the shelf behind the counter. All the crosses and lilies made him feel sick. A thousand sackfuls of cards couldn't bring Marigold back. But he, Fred Meecham, was going to preserve what they had had together and protect their secret until his own dying day. At any cost, he told himself.

The police had been to see him, turned up on the very night of Marigold's death. He had had no idea they could be so insensitive. Of course, later he realised they could not have known. They were polite and respectful and had not come to question him about the past at all but about Dorothy. He had told them when he had last seen her and that she had seemed in good spirits. What else was there to say? Then they had expressed interest in the drugs Marigold took. There were none in the house now, of course, he had handed them over as he had been asked to do, but he had had no trouble listing them. For two years he had supervised the taking of them. Then they had left. Fred had been shaken but also relieved. It was Dorothy they were interested in, not that other thing.

Fred was still convinced that money could have saved Marigold. He had not had enough of it and blamed himself rather man fate over which he had no control. Dorothy could have lent him some but she had refused.

Now it was over and Dorothy was dead too. In an odd

sort of way he missed her because she was a good listener and might have helped him deal with the pain. She was the one person who knew more about him and Marigold than anyone had. Both women had taken the secret with them to the grave.

Rose parked in a gateway, guessing that the farmer would not need to use it because there was stubble in the field and no more work would be done there until it was time for ploughing. Below her was the estuary, the tide low, the waders and gulls, settled in the middle, too far away to make out clearly. How Barry could be so sure she'd find the plant was a mystery but he must have done so himself or got someone else to because, after a wasted fifteen minutes, she finally saw the tiny delicate head of it and settled down to work. Not for much longer, Rose told herself as she held the drawing away from her to check it was exactly right.

She sat with her arms hugging her knees and looked at the small church on the brow of the hill, visualising it painted in oils. All right, she would finish all the jobs she had taken on then she would start again, see if she still had it in her to be a real artist. It had been too easy to accept the praises of Doreen Clarke and Barry Rowe. What was it Jack had said once? Yes, that his ex-wife had bought one of her oils because she had liked it, because it had feeling even if it wasn't technically a great piece of work. The technical side could be developed. Will be developed, Rose thought as she packed away her pencils. I will get my life sorted out and I will do my best for Dorothy.

Filled with determination she strode back to the car,

her hair flying in the wind. Water was flowing back into the estuary and many of the birds had disappeared in large flocks. A solitary egret proceeded to the waterline with queenly grace, its white plumage unmistakable. Once rare here, they were now often to be seen.

She reached the car and headed towards the main road, racking her brains as to what the warning had meant. It has to be somebody close, she thought, someone who knows I won't settle for less than the truth, someone who knows how much I cared about Dorothy.

It got her nowhere, less than a handful of people fell into that category and they were all people she trusted. Which reminded her, she had not been in touch with Jobber Hicks since their one conversation regarding Martin. He, too, would be lonely and missing Dorothy, his lifetime companion.

She sighed as she changed gear to pull into Dorothy's drive and the engine missed. 'You'll really have to go,' she told the Mini. There was no sign of Martin at the house so she walked over to the caravan. He wasn't there either and could be anywhere so it was pointless to wait. Standing on the hillside in the unnatural silence, Rose shivered. Clouds scudded across the sky, intermittently obscuring the sun. Their shadows passed stealthily over the grass, deadening its colour; their shapes sliding over the boulders seemed almost human. For the first time she began to wonder if Martin had anything to do with his mother's death: if someone had given her alcohol laced with enough drugs to kill her where had the mug or glass been? The table had been clear and the sink empty when she came upon the scene. Fear rose in her throat and she stifled an exclamation as a huge black cloud blocked out the light and turned the moorland into a place of evil where unseen eyes watched her. The cloud was blown southwards and she blinked in the sudden brightness. It was time to leave.

She did not see Peter Pengelly passing in the opposite direction as she made her way to where she intended to finish a piece of work because she did not recognise his car.

For two hours she continued without interruption. The threat of rain had passed and she could feel the autumnal warmth of the sun on her head. Gorse was still in its second flowering and bees hummed around the clover amongst which she was sitting. Putting aside her watercolours she lay back and closed her eyes, enjoying nothing but the colourful patterns which formed behind her lids. They reminded her of a kaleidoscope she had had as a child. A bee, black and gold like a Cornish rugby shirt, landed near her ear. Rose remained motionless whilst it went about its business. When it had flown off she sat up and poured coffee from her flask. Traffic was a distant murmur, not enough to disturb the peace. Ahead and surrounding her was nothing but scrubland with a few scruffy trees, but she felt no fear now. If it had not been for the brightness of the gorse she might have been on a hillside in Italy or Greece. Ah, yes, she thought, the gorse and the crumbling stack of a copper mine. Scattered the length and breadth of the county the old mines were so much a part of it, it was as if nature and not man was responsible for their presence.

With bent legs, knees splayed, Rose sat with the plastic cup of the flask held in both hands between them, her posture that of an unselfconscious teenager rather than a mature woman. Her denim skirt had slipped up her thighs exposing her tanned legs, the muscles toned by all the walking she did. Overhead a flash of silver caught her eye. It was a plane, reflecting the sun, too high for its engines to be heard and only visible because of the clarity of the air. In its wake was a vapour trail which was breaking up into white balls of fluff. 'Time to move,' she told herself, screwing the lid back on the flask and putting away her equipment. She shook dry seeds and grass from her clothes and strode back to the car. The almost smooth-stemmed Western Gorse, its flower more delicate than the everyday kind, had challenged her which was good, because she had a tendency to become complacent at times. The series would be complete before Barry actually required it. Tempting as it was to stay out of doors Rose knew there was more to be done at home. And the sooner it was done the sooner she could get out her oils.

There had been no message from Jack who was either still tied up at the station or too tired to want to see her. She did not contact him. Leaving the house at a few minutes to seven she arrived at Barry's promptly at seven thirty. He was flushed with a sheen of perspiration on his forehead. The sleeves of his white shirt were rolled up showing pale, freckled forearms gleaming with golden hairs. Over one shoulder was a tea towel and his glasses, perched on his nose, were faintly misted. He pushed them into place impatiently and kissed Rose chastely on the cheek. She was cool and smelt clean from her recent shower. He recognised the pale blue dress as the one she had bought on a trip to London with him and was flattered that she had worn it because he had said how much he liked it.

'I wish I hadn't attempted something so complicated. Help yourself to a drink, Rosie. This won't be ready for a while yet.' Barry turned back to the small counter upon which was a pile of dirty utensils.

'What're we having?' Rose reached for the wine bottle.

'Beef Wellington,' Barry replied with a touch of satisfaction as he wrapped shop-bought pastry around the meat he had spread with pâté.

'What? No pasta?'

'It's not the only thing I can cook,' he replied defensively.

'No, but it's the only thing which turns out right.'

'I shall ignore that. I'm simply trying to pay you back for the lovely things you cook for me.'

Rose handed him a glass of chilled white wine. 'Have a slurp of this before you explode.'

He did so, his fingers leaving greasy prints on the stem. Rose watched him struggle with the beef but was tactful enough not to say he could have bought the whole thing ready-made.

The kitchen was cramped and ill equipped. She took one of the two unmatching chairs and sat at the rickety table. Barry had lived in the one-bedroomed flat over the shop since she had known him. His financial status was of no concern to her but she knew that he could have afforded somewhere far better. He was, she decided, in a rut, but one in which he seemed content to remain.

'There! Or should I say *voilà?* It's in the oven. It might be an idea to drink ourselves senseless in case it's a disaster.

Right, now you can tell me what you've been up to.' The chair creaked beneath him as it took his weight.

'What makes you think I've been up to anything?' He looks so boyish and helpless at times, she thought. It's a shame no woman's got hold of him. 'I'm well ahead with the wild flowers. I did the Western Gorse this afternoon. It won't be long until they're all done. Why're you looking at me like that?'

'You're babbling, Rosie, and I know what that means.' He reached across the table and touched her hand. 'I didn't mean to upset you the other day, I know how you felt about Dorothy.'

Rose nodded and a loose hair fell on to her lap. She picked it off the material of her dress and wound it around her finger. 'I shall miss her. I'm already missing her.'

'I know.'

'The police said it was suicide, now they're not so sure but . . .' She shrugged and picked up her wineglass.

Barry's mouth tightened. By the police he assumed she meant Jack Pearce.

Correctly reading his expression Rose added, 'She didn't kill herself, Barry, I don't believe that for one minute. You don't think that, do you?'

'Oh, Rose.' Barry rubbed his forehead as if he was tired.

It had been best to get it over with before he heard from other sources and accused her of having secrets from him. This was the one aspect of his character which infuriated her. If she told him things he accused her of meddling, if she did not he called her secretive. Rose then announced that she would not be readily available for commercial

121

work, she was reverting to oils. The expected outburst did not come.

'At last,' Barry said, smiling.

'Don't you mind?'

'Mind? Good God, Rosie, why should I? It's your life, your career and, to tell you the truth, I was disappointed when you didn't keep going. You see, I always thought you'd improve. Each one was always slightly better man the last. Go for it, that's what I say.'

She could barely believe what she was hearing but the encouragement was worth more than any commission. Her desire was now not to let Barry down. 'Oh, and I've been invited to a party on Saturday.'

'Oh? The glasses were pushed up once more, this time the gesture was deliberate, to disguise what would show in his face when Rose said that Pearce was taking her. 'Why're you grinning?'

'Because I can read your mind.' She twirled her glass between her fingers knowing that she was teasing him. 'I'm going by myself.'

'I see.' No Jack, he thought, but no Barry either.

'My social life's becoming as restricted as yours. I miss the times when I was mixing with other artists and writers. I have to do something about it.'

Barry nodded. She was right. They talked of general things until it was time to serve the meal. It was far better than either of them had anticipated and they ate the lot. 'I think I'll walk home rather man get a cab,' Rose said.

'And I shall accompany you. I need to walk it off, too.'

There was a three-quarter moon illuminating the bay.

Pale ripples spread into the surrounding blackness of the water. The lights of Newlyn were to their right when they stopped to lean over the railing to absorb the sound of the sea sucking at the pebbles. Rose thought she could listen to it for ever. The distinctive cry of a curlew reached them as it took off from Larrigan rocks which were completely visible now the tide was out. 'Come on, we'd better make a move.'

Arm in arm they walked along past the Bowls Club, situated right on the front and exposed to the elements, past the Newlyn Gallery and around to tine Strand and the now shuttered fish market then up the hill. To their left the harbour was lit by moonlight and the lifeboat, *Mabel Alice,* lay slightly on one side as the incoming tide lapped at her hull, gently nudging her upright.

Barry left Rose at her door then began the return journey. He chewed his mouth thoughtfully, knowing that if there was anything unusual about Dorothy Pengelly's death Rose would not rest until she had found out what it was. Better to think of that than Jack Pearce or whom she might meet at Mike and Barbara's party.

Rose threw her shoulder bag into an armchair. The clasp had been undone and the contents spilt out on to the floor. She ignored them and kicked off her shoes, always preferring to be barefoot in the house. The evening had gone well and Barry's reaction to her involvement with the Pengelly family had not been as censorious as she had expected. In fact, he had surprised her in several ways.

The sitting-room was half lit by the moon and the light from the hall. Rose turned to take one last look at the bay as she did every night. As she left the room she saw the red light of the answering machine winking in the corner. Jack, she thought. Her brow creased in a frown when she heard Jobber's voice. He had started the message twice, the second time was clearer. It was too late to contact him or Martin now so she would do as he had asked and meet them in the morning. Was it too late to ring Jack? She was surprised he had not been in touch, if only to find out if she had been to see the Pengellys. 'No, bugger him,' she muttered and went upstairs to bed.

CHAPTER SEVEN

Jobber Hicks had got into his ramshackle van and made his way slowly to Dorothy's house. He had not wanted to burden Martin with his request too soon because the boy might give him an answer he would later regret. He always drove at a leisurely pace because he saw no reason to rush through life. The end would come at some point. Happily ignoring impatient drivers behind him he slowed to take the bend then indicated right, turning into Dorothy's drive.

Jobber's calloused and roughened hands gripped the wheel at precisely ten to three, the way his father had taught him, and his head, tortoise-like, jutted forward from the loose collar of his shirt as he peered through the windscreen. His lack of height did not bother him. All his family had been short. The skin of his face, neck and forearms was weathered but the rest of his body had not seen the sun since childhood. Only in repose did the starburst of lines around his eyes relax enough to reveal the paler skin in the creases. His grey hair was cropped short and he wore whatever happened to be nearest when he got dressed. All his clothes held a faint suggestion of manure.

The van was worse. It stank of animals. Often a single sheep or pig was loaded into the back of it to be taken to market. For more than one he used the horsebox.

He killed the ignition and let the silence fill his ears, half expecting Dorothy to come to the door. Jobber studied the sky and nodded knowledgeably. It would rain before the day was out. He, like his father before him, could predict the weather with more accuracy than any satellite station.

Leaving the van where it was, he walked around the side of the house and peered through the kitchen window. The dogs were there, in their usual places. Star was scratching behind her ear in an ungainly fashion. They looked restful and their bowls were empty. Martin must have seen to them already.

Jobber continued on up the hill, his pace so steady his heartbeat did not alter. In the distance, slumped against a boulder, he spotted Martin. He waited until he was near enough to talk in a normal voice before he spoke.

Martin raised his face. He looked haggard. 'He came back,' he said.

'Who did? Who came back?'

'The bugger I saw in the pub.'

Jobber's eyes narrowed. What had Martin been saying to this stranger? 'Have you told the police, son?' Jobber, too, had been questioned and was aware that things might not be as straightforward as everyone had initially believed.

'No.' Martin got to his feet. His nostrils were pinched and he was white around the mouth. 'Won't bring 'er back, will 'un?'

'No. Nothing's going to do that. Why don't us go on

down to the house. There's something I want to ask you.' He thought Martin looked in need of a strong mug of tea.

Together they negotiated the irregular route back down. The dogs greeted them both in a friendly way and Jobber put the kettle on. They drank the tea black. 'Are you coping?' Jobber nodded towards the animals.

'They're no trouble. I take 'em out twice a day and feed the cats.'

Jobber leant forward. 'Martin, do you think I could have Star? I'd look after her proper, like, you can rest assured of that. I'll even pay you for 'un, if you've a mind.'

Martin stared at the Greyhound. There was no room for her in his van and if she went to the farm she'd have company. 'All right. I don't want no money, though.'

They sipped their tea in silence. Both were men of few words. 'I should stay here, at the house. He'll come back again else.'

'Who is this man you keep on about? If you think he's trouble you've got to tell the police.' Jobber's hands shook. If Martin was right he had no need to feel any guilt. He had cried in the belief that he might have driven Dorothy to her death, unaware that he had not been as persistent as he thought, that a lot of it had been in his head.

'No. I'll tell Mrs Trevelyan. ''Er'll know what to do.'

Jobber nodded. Rose Trevelyan was a sensible woman and had been more than a good friend to Dorothy. Good-looking with it, too, he thought. He nodded again and ran a hand around his badly shaved chin. Although he had had few dealings with the police he had an inborn prejudice against them. 'We could telephone her now.'

'You do it.'

Jobber glanced at his watch. It was getting on for seven o'clock. Mrs Trevelyan would probably be at home. He found the number in the book beside the telephone and felt a sharp pain in his chest seeing Dorothy's large, rounded writing. He began speaking before he realised he was talking to a recorded message. 'Damn things,' he said, feeling stupid and self-conscious. Clearing his throat he stood straighter as if Rose's disembodied voice was able to see him. He said that Martin had something important to tell her and asked if she was free to come to Dorothy's house at ten the next morning. 'Thank you,' he said politely at the end of the message. 'There, all done. That just leaves the problem of Star.'

They loaded half of the tins of dog food and her blanket and basket into the back of the van, then finally Star herself. Martin patted her fondly and watched as Jobber turned around and drove to the end of the lane.

Star whined and fretted and rested her front paws on the back of Jobber's seat where he had left the dividing window open. He spoke to her soothingly and quietly. Star would settle down in a day or two. Jobber had had many dogs in his life and knew their ways well.

Fred Meecham sat with his head in his hands, his red hair sticking up untidily. The vicar had shown no surprise that his sister's surname was different from his own, it was known that she had been through a bad marriage. Marigold Heath was the name on her death certificate. No one had yet asked to see this certificate. The woman who had issued it at the register office had needed nothing other than the form from the hospital doctor who had pronounced her to be dead.

Her headstone would be simple, bearing only her name and her dates and his own contribution, 'always loved'. Fred did not know what to do about her other relatives, or even if they were alive. Time was running out and many things were preying on his mind. Both Marigold and Dorothy would have known what to do but they were no longer in a position to help him.

Jack Pearce was not in the best of moods, which irritated him as much as anyone else. The whole thing was shambolic but he couldn't blame the officers who had been the first at the scene. Dorothy Pengelly had been an old lady who had died accidentally or deliberately from an overdose. The police surgeon had seen it almost immediately and this had been confirmed by the pathologist. There had been no need for the murder team. He still wasn't as convinced as Rose that it was anything else and any evidence, if it was evidence, had been destroyed. The paracetamol bottle had disappeared and any container in which the drug had been administered would have been washed up. They could still fingerprint the place but what would that show? Martin and Rose had keys, old prints were likely to have been disturbed or smudged and they only had Rose's say-so on who might have been in the house.

Was there a will? Was money the motive? If there has been a crime, Jack reminded himself. If Dorothy was intestate both sons would inherit equally, if there was a will it might be a different matter but murdering her would not alter its contents. If one or other son stood to gain little he would want her alive in order to have a chance of persuading her to change it. But the reverse was also true. Supposing Dorothy had left everything to one son but had been about to change her own mind? And where was the painting? One of her children must have it. He shook his head in exasperation. Here, too, was information based only on Rose's opinion. Jack warned himself to be careful. He must not let his professional judgement be clouded because he trusted the instincts of Rose Trevelyan.

Interviewing the family had been a waste of time. No one had a decent alibi but why should they have if they were innocent? Peter and Gwen claimed to have been together watching television all evening and had gone to bed around eleven. With two small children this was more than likely true. Martin said he had been alone, in his van. Either he was totally honest or he knew they would not be able to prove otherwise.

Jobber Hicks and Fred Meecham, apparently Dorothy's only other friends, had also been questioned. Meecham's sister had just died and he was understandably too upset to be of much help. Jobber, Jack knew from Rose, was Dorothy's ardent admirer and he could see no reason why he should wish her dead.

I'm wasting my time, he thought as the day drew to a close. The old lady decided she had had enough of life. It's as simple as that.

Three times during the evening he dialled Rose's number only to get the answering machine. He could have left a message but what he really wanted was to speak to her in person. Strange that she should be avoiding him, unless she knew something she didn't want him to know just yet. That wouldn't surprise him at all. But he was unaware that Rose was spending the evening in the company of Barry Rowe, the man whom he considered to be his rival.

Fred Meecham was trying desperately hard to get on with the everyday running of his shop. It was a delivery day and, at least for the morning, the added work helped take his mind off Marigold. He checked the forms against what he had ordered then unpacked the goods and restacked the shelves although this was usually the job of one of his part-time assistants. Beneath his red hair his face was whiter than usual. He realised that these were still early days, that at some unspecified point in the future he would come to terms with it all and live normally again. For now his grief and anger were eating away at him.

When customers spoke he answered them as best he could, aware of the glances which passed between them and the assistant behind me counter.

Life had dealt him two harsh blows where women were concerned, first the departure of his wife with the young sales rep and now Marigold. On top of this his son was an ingrate, unappreciative of the sacrifices Fred had made for him. He had not seen him for years now and Fred was not sorry.

He had always stuck to the rules, done things by the book, and it had got him nowhere. During those first years with his ex-wife he had borne with stoicism the endless rows and her avarice, never resorting to violence or taking consolation elsewhere. She had repaid him by moving out and leaving their son behind. That son, too, had gone.

Abandoned now for the third time Fred went through the motions. He collected up the empty cardboard boxes and took them out to the back where he would later burn them. He needed some air and to spend a few minutes away from the shop. Pounding away in his head was the idea that he had deserved all he had got, but there had only been two aberrations in his life. One had given him immeasurable pleasure, the second nothing but a fleeting minute's joy followed by a hopeless rage.

He returned to the shop, picked up a price gun and began marking tins of corned beef.

Biting her lip, Rose tried unsuccessfully to arrange her hair in a neat roll at the back of her head. She claimed she kept it shoulder-length because there was so much more she could do with it, something about which Laura teased her. 'You've either got it loose or in a ponytail,' she said. But Laura wasn't there to admire her effort when she finally got it right.

It was not so much her hair which bothered her at that moment but herself. She was sometimes gregarious and other people's lives and personalities fascinated her but, like Martin Pengelly, she required stretches of isolation. This was one of the reasons she had not been able to make a commitment to Jack and she recognised it as a fault. She had known she would not mourn for ever and had enough insight to see that she had used Jack as the first stage in her recovery. Laura had it both ways. Trevor, at home to enjoy and fuss over, then periods of a week or ten days when he was at sea. And now, when she needed some breathing space, she would not allow herself any because she was worried sick about Martin. Yet her feelings were ambiguous. One minute she wanted to protect him, the next to put as much distance between them as possible. She was, as Barry would have pointed out, becoming too involved. Martin worried her in various ways but Jobber would be there too.

It had rained overnight and the road was still damp. The clouds, a curving canopy of grey, domed over the sea. The salvage tug which came and went was once more anchored in the bay after refuelling in Falmouth. It pitched and tossed on white-capped waves.

The Mini was buffeted as she picked up speed on the main road and the canvas cover of a high-sided lorry flapped noisily as it passed her going in the opposite direction. Knowing flocks of gulls drifted inland and took refuge in the fields.

The blank windows of Dorothy's house reflected the car as she drew up in front of it. Jobber's old van was already there, parked on the grass to allow her room.

He appeared at the side of the building as she stepped out into the blustery morning. 'We've made the tea,' he said by way of greeting. 'I'm glad you could make it, Mrs Trevelyan. Martin's in a bit of a state.'

She followed him around to the back door, neither of them wishing to presume to use the front one. The wind whipped at her clothes as they turned the corner.

Martin was sitting at the kitchen table. He seemed to have shrunk further and there were dark shadows under his eyes. Despite his Spartan living conditions he kept himself clean and tidy. He wore jeans and shirt and a V-necked jumper and his durable boots. His brown hair was neatly combed.

'Where's Star?' Rose asked, surprised to see that the space her basket usually occupied was empty.

'I've taken her. She's a bit restless, but she'll soon get used to the place. I didn't bring 'un this morning, though, it'd only confuse her.'

It was Jobber who poured Rose's treacle-coloured tea, adding milk which he had brought from the farm. She waited, wondering which one of them would be the first to speak. Martin's eyes were dull, his expression flat as he stared at the mug in front of him. 'Martin? Was there something you wanted to tell me?' she asked, half expecting another admission.

He finally looked up but remained silent. Jobber nudged him. 'Go on, tell her, tell Mrs Trevelyan.'

'They're back. The two men I told you about. One of them was hanging around outside the house. He didn't know I was about. I told 'un, I said if I ever caught him here again I'd kill him.' Some colour had returned to his face. 'I nearly hit him.' He picked up his mug and drank deeply.

'Who are these men?' Rose looked at Jobber who raised his shoulders to show he knew no more than she did.

'I met them down Hayle. In the pub. We had some drinks.' Martin's face darkened further as he recalled just how many drinks and how he had been foolish enough to let one of the men pay for some of them. 'We got talking. I said . . . I said Mum had some nice stuff an' he told me he went round buying off people.' He stopped, ashamed that the drinks had made him boastful. 'If I hadn't said that, they wouldn't have killed her.' He bowed his head and Rose finally understood what had been troubling him.

'Do you think they were con men, Martin? Do you think they came here and frightened your mother?'

'Yeah. Something like that, I suppose.'

'Mrs Trevelyan?' Jobber had seen the look of horror on Rose's face. She was thinking about the Stanhope Forbes and what men like that might do to get hold of one. Realising his incomprehension she explained to Jobber about the painting.

'Dorothy owned one?'

Martin was watching them both. He had no idea why they were making such a fuss over one of Dorothy's pictures. It had hung on the wall ever since he could remember and, as far as he knew, no one had commented on it, least of all his mother. And if it was worth so much money, why hang it in the bedroom where only she could see it? Martin had known about the bits of china but he had been unaware that paintings could be expensive. Of course, Mrs Trevelyan would know because she was clever in that way.

'But there's a reproduction hanging in its place now,' Rose concluded. There was no reason why Jobber should have known, Dorothy was not a boastful woman.

'I knew she had some valuable paintings, but she never mentioned no names. Did you tell the police, Mrs Trevelyan?'

'Yes. I had to. Martin hadn't realised because he never went in that room.'

'Don't matter now, boy, we've got to tell the police.'

'I already did, the first time. I told 'un I thought I'd spoke out of turn because they were strangers.'

Rose frowned. She did not know they had been to see Martin at all. But she saw why he was upset. He believed himself responsible for bringing the men to the house in the first place, if that was what had happened. It was all conjecture, of course – they may not have been near the place and if they had, they may have left Dorothy in perfect health. She was beginning to wonder if she had made a terrible mistake only because she didn't want to believe it of Dorothy. But Rose still couldn't help asking, 'Did you tell these men where the house was?'

His blush answered the question. Rose met Jobber's eyes and each knew what the other was thinking. 'And you saw one of them again. When was that?'

'Yesterday. That's when I threatened 'im.'

It was puzzling. If someone had cheated Dorothy and, in the process, felt the need to silence her, it was unlikely that they would return. 'Martin, when did they come? The first time, I mean?'

'I don't know. I never saw them then.'

'Look, we have to be very careful. If you didn't see them, yesterday might've been the first visit. The man would have no reason to know that . . .' She stopped. There was no point in making things harder for Martin.

'Could be. Could be that he came back for more of what wasn't 'is.'

Martin had a point. 'Would you know them again, boy?'

'Course I would.' He gave Jobber a strange look. He wasn't daft. But he did not realise that Jobber had had an idea.

'He says they're not local, so if they're not from round here and he met them in the pub and now they seem to be back again, well, you can see how the land might lie.'

Rose thought she was following what Jobber was getting

136

at. 'You think they might be staying at the same place in which case we could find them?'

'That's exactly what I was thinking, Mrs Trevelyan.' He sucked his unlit pipe.

'Oh, Jobber, please call me Rose.'

'An' as pretty as one too, to my eyes.'

Rose was more flattered than she would have been had another male offered her the banal compliment. Jobber did not waste words on things he did not mean. 'Thank you. Look, why don't we meet later, say about six, and see if Martin can point them out to us.' Rose swallowed the guilt she felt knowing that she ought to have told Jack about the men even if they had been a figment of Martin's imagination. I will, she promised, later this evening.

They arranged to meet at Jobber's farm. Rose would collect the two of them there as the van only had the two seats in the front.

'And that'll give Martin a chance to take a look at Star. Here, why don't you come a bit earlier, boy, and have a bite of supper with me?'

Martin said he would and Rose was touched by the older man's concern. 'What's going to happen to George?'

'Well, now, I've had an idea or two about that, too,' Jobber replied but refused to expand upon it. The Jack Russell growled as if he was aware he was under discussion but since Dorothy's death and now the disappearance of Star some of his aggression had left him. The dog was the most unlovable pet Rose had come across but the cats were even worse. They were almost feral and hissed and spat if anyone but Dorothy went near them.

No further words were exchanged as they each went their separate ways. Rose wondered when she would hear from Jack and how much she would tell him if he rang before she left home again that evening.

Several hardy souls were battling their way across the Promenade, heading into the wind on the raised pavement opposite the Mount's Bay Inn. Their lightweight jackets billowed around them. If the wind was coming from the west there was a chance of more rain but she would be home long before it started.

There were two messages from Jack. The first said he would try again later, the second asked her to contact him at the station as soon as she got home. She tried but was told he wasn't available. Rose left her own message with a sergeant then went upstairs to develop some rolls of film.

'Goddamn the woman,' Jack said when he returned to his office and found the note on the desk. He still had no idea how her meeting with the Pengellys had gone or if she had been there at all. Once more he rang her number and was relieved to hear her voice.

'That's it?' he asked, disappointed when she had given her explanation.

'Yes. Sorry, Jack.'

'You did your best.'

Rose was glad he could not see her. He would have known by her face that there was more but she was not ready to tell him yet. After the trip to Hayle later would be the time to tell him whether or not anything came of it.

Perverting the course of justice? Obstructing the law? she asked herself, having replaced the receiver. No, she

138

amended, more like bloody-mindedness. If Jack was doing his job properly he would know all about the nameless men in Hayle.

Rose was unaware that the landlord of the pub had already been questioned but was unable to supply the names because they had paid for their accommodation in advance, in cash, which might indicate that the transaction did not go through the books but was of no help in identifying them.

CHAPTER EIGHT

Bradley Hinkston stood at the bar with a brandy and soda in his hand, more shaken now than he had been yesterday. How right his initial instincts about the Pengelly family had been. Eccentric was not a strong enough word to describe them. The old lady must have been having him on in some way, although he couldn't quite see how, not after his first visit. Then, out of the blue, he had been physically threatened by the son. The only thing to do now was forget all about it and pack up and go home. Too late tonight. He'd been drinking and Louise was not expecting him because he had telephoned to say he was staying on. Besides, he'd already paid for a second night and he couldn't expect the landlord to give him his money back.

Tomorrow he intended visiting a village near Plymouth for a house clearance sale. From the catalogue he did not think it would be very profitable but there were a few nice pieces he wouldn't mind if he could beat the other dealers to them. What annoyed him most was that if he had been able to get his hands on Mrs Pengelly's other paintings and that

140

rather nice commode it would have added to his reputation as far as his customers were concerned. With a mental shrug he decided to put it all behind him and enjoy the home-made steak and kidney pudding and fresh vegetables which were offered on the menu. He would have another drink to settle his nerves before he ordered. Louise tended to go for exotic foods or things which would not harm her figure. Alone, Bradley allowed himself to indulge in large helpings of plain cooking.

He moved away from the bar as more customers came in. He wanted to be sure of a table at which to eat. When a gust of wind told him that the door had been opened again he looked up automatically. 'Oh, Lord,' he whispered. It was the Pengelly boy and he had come with reinforcements. He hoped there would not be some awful public scene. However, the short, grizzled man and the extremely attractive middle-aged woman posed no real threat. It was the son who might be out for trouble. He placed a finger to his lips as he wondered what the disparate group wanted.

As they went up to the bar and ordered drinks he saw them whispering.

It was the woman who approached the table first, the two men close behind her. In the car they had decided that they had been stupid, that there was no chance of the men being there. Now they were actually facing one of them no one was sure what to do.

Rose quickly took in the debonair man who looked completely at ease. He reminded her of a fifties film star she was unable to name. The silver hair and well-defined features were attractive. Neither Jobber nor Martin appeared to want to initiate conversation so it was left to her. 'Excuse us interrupting, but we're friends of Mrs Pengelly. Well, two of us are,' she began uncertainly. 'This is Jobber Hicks. And this is her son, Martin. I believe you've already met.'

Bradley had not been expecting such polite introductions. He turned on his full charm. 'Jobber, what an interesting name. And Hicks. Don't tell me you're responsible for that excellent local beer by the same name?'

'No, I'm a farmer. We'd like to know who you are.'

'Forgive me. Won't you sit down?' He waved a hand over the empty seats surrounding him. 'It's so relaxing down here it's easy to forget one's manners.' He stood as they joined his table. 'I'm Bradley Hinkston and I'm very pleased to meet you.'

Rose introduced herself as his eyes slid appreciatively down to her legs.

Bradley sipped his drink. 'Mr Pengelly, I'm pleased that we're now on better terms. Unless, of course, this is your hit-team?'

The incongruity of the comment and the man's wry humour amused Rose. Jobber took it more seriously. 'Martin meant nothing by his behaviour, sir. Naturally, he was upset.'

'Yes. It must've appeared as if I was trespassing, but Mrs Pengelly—'

'Just a minute.' Rose stopped him. Unless he was a true con artist he did not know that Dorothy was dead. 'Mr Hinkston, Martin's mother died on Thursday night.'

'What? Oh, my goodness'. I'm so sorry. No wonder—' but he stopped himself that time. 'Oh, dear, I should've telephoned first.'

'Wouldn't've been no point. She couldn't have answered,' Martin stated philosophically.

'I can't believe it, she was fine when I last saw her.'

So he had been to the house before and he was making no attempt to hide the fact. This, Rose knew, would be important to the police, more so in view of his next comment.

'Thursday! I was with her on Thursday. I didn't know she was ill, she really showed no signs of being so. Oh, dear. If only she'd said.'

'Would you mind us knowing what it was you went to see her about?' Jobber had taken the initiative.

'I don't know what all this is about, but would you allow me to freshen your drinks before we continue?'

Rose and Jobber said yes but Martin put a hand firmly over his glass. He knew what had happened the last time. 'Why not, 'e looks like 'e's got a few bob,' Jobber whispered but Martin shook his head.

Bradley returned with the glasses then leant back in his seat ready to answer their questions, not admitting that he was as baffled as his interviewers. They listened, astonished, to what he had to tell them. Later, in the car, Martin surprised them. A will existed and he knew where it was.

It was nine thirty before Bradley got to eat his steak and kidney pudding, and it gave him indigestion. Foolishly he had ignored his instinct which had told him not to return.

'No,' Peter Pengelly stated firmly. 'You are not going up there. The solicitors'll sort it out. Knowing Mother, everything will be in order.'

'But it needs a good clean.'

Peter knew Gwen's intention was to remove anything she thought to be of value, small things, maybe, but nonetheless, they were not hers to take. He still could not understand the urgency: they both believed that the bulk of the estate was coming to them. If Gwen feared Martin had the same intention as herself she need not have worried. His brother was completely trustworthy.

Peter turned his head as he heard the swish of his wife's legs crossing. Her skirt had slid higher up and the top of one stocking was visible, as he knew it was meant to be. He sighed. Did she really think her blatant methods would work now? Was she incapable of seeing that he was still grieving? Even allowing for her miserable childhood he was impatient with her.

Peter's grim face showed Gwen she had made the wrong move. She tugged her skirt into place and sat up straight. 'I didn't mean anything by it, Peter, I just thought if the house had a good clean it would be easier to sell. I keep meaning to ask you, do you know where the will actually is?'

'No. But her solicitors or the bank probably have the original.'

'I don't mean to sound mercenary, but they won't necessarily know she's dead, not unless we tell them.'

He frowned. It was true. It was the first sensible suggestion she had made. It was up to the relatives to make it known. 'I'll see to it in the morning. Failing that I'll get the key off Martin and we'll look for it together.'

Gwen's face relaxed.

'Me and Martin, I meant.'

Gwen saw there was no point in arguing.

* * *

Rose unlocked the kitchen door. She was much later than she had anticipated. The hall was lit, the timer switch had come on a couple of hours ago. It had been Jack's idea and he had installed it for her. It was yet another reminder of the way she had allowed him into her life.

Locking the door behind her she reached out for the kitchen light switch then boiled a kettle for tea. At the moment the idea of sleep was impossible. There was so much else to think about and she ought to ring Jack immediately. There were several messages for her but they all concerned work. Rose made a note of the numbers. She would return the calls but it was doubtful if she would take on the jobs. Leaving a message for Jack on his answering machine she went to bed. Her sleep was patchy and she dreamt of the life she had stayed in Cornwall for, where her friends were talented or bohemian or both, and their minds were intellectual. Deep sleep only came before dawn and she awoke feeling drained, but the first thing she did was to get out her oil paints.

At eight she rang Jack's flat only to find she had missed him. He was not at his desk at work either. She did not leave a message.

Rose made a list of the things she needed to do: a trip to the library, some grocery shopping, a dozen rolls of fast film and some business cards to collect from the printers; mundane chores after her grand plans, but they had to be done. After that, coffee with Laura whom she felt she had been neglecting.

With her books in a carrier and her bag slung diagonally across her body, Rose set off for Penzance. Once all the items were ticked off her list she still had twenty minutes to spare so she decided to call in at the book shop in Chapel Street to order an illustrated art book she had seen reviewed in the paper. It was her favourite street. Dog-legged at the bottom and steeply sloped, it was lined with historic buildings, including the Union Hotel from where news of the death of Nelson was first announced. Further down, the pavements were high and cobbled and so narrow that two people could not walk abreast.

She ordered the book then walked up Causewayhead where they were to meet. Ahead of her were three young people, travellers, as they were now called. It was the way in which they were dressed which caught her eye, the multi-coloured layers of the girls' clothing and their beaded plaits. She had dressed in a similar manner in her own youth.

'Look.' Laura nudged her and smirked.

Rose jumped, she hadn't seen her approach. She followed Laura's gaze.

'Why do they do it?' A middle-aged man in loud Bermuda shorts was accompanied by a woman his own age in a pastel lemon towelling tracksuit through which the bulges of her flesh were visible.

'Holiday gear.' Many tourists were so predictable. Rose saw the parallel with her own life.

'Why the dark glasses?' Rose asked when they were seated in the cafe and had ordered their coffee. 'Afraid you'll be recognised?' Trevor was at sea so they had not had one of their rows which left Laura tear-stained.

Laura removed them. 'That's why. Both my sons arrived last night and we had a bit of a pub crawl. I feel a little poorly this morning.'

'Yon look it. But it serves you right.'

'Don't be smug, Rose, dear. You're not exactly abstemious yourself. It wouldn't surprise me if you've got shares in a vineyard. Shall we have something to eat?'

'Not for me.'

'Are you okay? I didn't mean to be flippant.' She knew Rose must still be thinking about Dorothy.

'I'm worried, Laura, none of it seems right. Anyway, I've got other things to tell you.'

'You want to prove something to Jack.'

They had been friends for years, since they were in their early twenties, and could say almost anything to each other without causing offence.

'Maybe, but it's more than that. However, Jack's no longer part of the equation.'

'What? He's quite a dish, Rose. Why not just enjoy what you've got?' Laura replaced the sunglasses to hide her astonishment.

'I don't want to any more.'

'He's crazy about you, Rose. Are you afraid of taking a second chance? I've noticed that every time you seem to be getting closer you distance yourself from him. He'd try to make you happy, you know.'

'Yes, he'd try but it wouldn't work if I don't want it. And you're always saying you shouldn't rely on other people to provide your happiness. So, how are the boys?'

Laura began to understand that her friend had finally pulled through. It had been a long haul but she had got there. She chatted about her sons and their families, animated when she spoke of their achievements. Watching her, so full of vitality even after a heavy night out, Rose found it hard to believe that there were two generations growing up behind her. Laura's life was full and she was contented, but in a different way from the way Rose wanted.

When they left the cafe Rose found an outfit to wear to Barbara and Mike's party and said she would have it without looking at the price tags. It was unlike any of the clothes in her existing wardrobe.

The phone rang as soon as she got back. Jack wanted to see her immediately. Rose plugged in the percolator but she did not offer him anything to eat when he arrived just before one.

'We seem to keep missing each other. Did you have a chance to speak to Martin?'

She leant back against the rounded edge of the worktop and folded her arms. No hello, no kiss, nothing but The Job. Under the circumstances her annoyance was ridiculous. 'Yes. I ran your errands for you, Jack.'

He squinted at her quizzically. 'Teasy today, aren't we?'

'Are we? I don't know. What I do know is that I'm sick and tired of not having a minute to myself.' She turned her back and fiddled with the coffee pot. He had not really deserved that and she disliked herself for her sharpness, it was out of character. It was going to be difficult to finish it. 'Sugar?' Unable to soften her tone she pushed the bowl towards him, then sat down herself. 'I told you on the phone that seeing Peter and Gwen was a waste of time. She didn't seem particularly upset although I'm pretty certain she is worried about something. I think Gwen's main concern is what's in the will.'

'The will?' Jack looked surprised.

'Yes. And they're not just guessing. I know for a fact that one exists.'

'All right, Rose, let's hear it all.' He leant forward, his deep blue eyes on her face. She lowered her head because when he looked at her like that it did something strange to her stomach.

'We'd just finished talking to Bradley Hinkston when Martin told us he knew where the will was kept. Dorothy's solicitors have it, and Martin seems to think they're the executors too. He says his mother didn't keep a copy in the house but he doesn't know why.'

'Martin told you? I would've thought – never mind. But who the hell is Bradley Hinkston?'

'Well, it was like this.' She took a deep breath then carefully explained from the beginning, from the time Jobber had telephoned her. Jack listened in amazement at the plan they had formed and how successful it had been.

'The Three bloody Musketeers. As I've said before, you really do slay me, Mrs Trevelyan. Go on.'

There had been admiration in his voice. 'The will first. Martin's positive about it because he went with her to Truro when she drew it up and again when she signed it, although he was made to wait outside.'

Jack wrote down the name of the solicitor in question. 'That's great, we can take it from there. Now this Hinkston bloke.'

Rose drained the last of her coffee and went to pour more. Jack held out his mug. He was familiar with all her actions and this one, the ritual refilling, was, in Rose's case, much the same thing as someone rolling up their sleeves ready to get stuck in.

'Bradley Hinkston is an antiques dealer from Bristol. He has an assistant called Roy Phelps. Someone else usually runs the shop while they go out buying and selling. Occasionally they are asked for a specific object and Bradley says that's the part he enjoys most, the search for whatever it is a customer wants. They also do valuations.'

Jack sat back, crossed his long legs at the ankles and folded his arms. He was impressed.

'Purely by chance, or so he says, they came across Martin when he turned up at the pub in which they were staying. They got chatting and Martin, a bit the worse for wear, started boasting about his mother's possessions once he knew what line of work they were in. They bought him more drinks. Now I don't know whether this was to loosen his vocal chords further or whether there was a more innocent explanation.' Rose looked thoughtful. 'He didn't strike me as a dishonest man, but that's only my opinion, for what it's worth.'

Your opinion is extremely valuable to me, Jack thought, and you're a damn good judge of character. 'So Hinkston hot tails it out to the Pengelly place to do Dorothy out of her paintings or whatever.'

'Not according to him. He says after he spoke to Martin he looked up the number and address in the phone book and contacted her first. He put his cards on the table and she invited him out there. Naturally Bradley was interested, who wouldn't be? But he wasn't sure if Martin was telling the complete truth. Dorothy gave him a warm welcome and said something along the lines about his having come at the right time. He couldn't believe his luck. He said she offered him the Stanhope Forbes and that she had a pretty good idea how much it was worth. There was, however, one proviso. He had to find her a replica. He got one that day, they're not hard to come by.'

'Come off it, Rose. You surely didn't fall for that?'

'Why not? He says he paid her by cheque. There'll be a record of it somewhere.'

'But why did she want the picture replaced?'

'That's the thing. She wanted him to come back as soon as he could and buy more stuff from her but all under the same conditions. She didn't want her family to know anything was missing. And again according to Bradley, it was to do with her will.'

'I don't understand. If she'd made one, however she divided her estate, selling her possessions wouldn't make any difference.'

Rose shrugged and brushed back her hair. 'I know. You'll have to get the will to find out.'

'We'd already asked questions at the pub,' Jack said to fill the silence which followed Rose's last statement. He vaguely resented it, it was as if she was telling him how to do his job. 'The landlord wasn't any help. He knew we wanted to speak to those men – he should have got in touch when they came back.'

'Only one of them came back and he went out to Dorothy's for a second time.' Rose paused. 'The day before yesterday.'

Jack's mouth dropped open and Rose could not help smiling. One to me, Jack Pearce, she thought, and here

151

comes a second one. She opened her bag which was hanging over the back of her chair. 'Bradley Hinkston's business card. In case you wanted to speak to him.'

Jack stared at it, then at Rose who was unable to hide a smirk. He nodded as he placed the card in his inside jacket pocket. 'I suppose you know how grateful I am?'

'Naturally, and with justification.'

'Then you also know you should have told me all this before, as soon as you went to Dorothy's and Martin told you Hinkston had come back.'

'What difference would it have made?' Trust you, she thought. Maybe he'd like to charge her with something. But deep down she knew he was right.

'It would have saved us a day. Is there anything else you haven't told me?'

'No. That's it. I thought I ought to leave some of it to our wonderful boys in blue.'

'Sarcasm doesn't become you, Rose.'

'No. But you were the one who suggested I go and see Peter, you're the one who got me involved and you obviously know a lot of things which you can't tell me. One day won't make any difference, Jack, not to Dorothy anyway.' To her consternation Rose found she was crying. The tears came without warning because it had suddenly hit her that she would never see Dorothy again.

'Oh, Rose. Don't. Please.'

He got up and went around to her side of the table where she sat with her face in her hands and gently touched the back of her neck beneath her hair. He had forgotten that feelings were involved, that Rose had been Dorothy's friend. Nothing seemed important other than that she stopped crying and told him it was not all over between them. Hinkston was an honest man, Dorothy had killed herself, Dorothy had been murdered, he would believe anything if it meant not losing Rose.

Rose straightened up. 'I'm sorry. It's a long time since I've made such a fool of myself.' Her voice was cold. 'There's nothing else I can tell you so you might as well leave.'

'No.' He knelt on the flagstone floor. 'No, Rose, I won't leave until you say I can see you again.'

'And if I don't?'

He raised his palms helplessly. 'Then I don't know what I'd do,' he said very quietly.

Rose wiped away a last tear with her index finger. 'Give me a ring this evening. I need to be on my own right now.'

He stood and walked slowly to the door. It wasn't a definite no, he had to be content with that.

When he'd gone Rose cried again, her head on the table as the hot tears of release flowed down her face. She had not realised how tense she was and how hard it would be to say goodbye to Jack. Not that she had done so yet. It was also a relief to hand everything over to him. But she had forgotten to tell him about the telephone call. She had almost forgotten it herself. Bradley Hinkston? Why not? Perhaps Dorothy had mentioned her name, or Martin for that matter. More likely Martin, who may have built her up out of all proportion. But why would Bradley think that Rose would not be satisfied with a suicide verdict? And hadn't she told Jack she thought he was honest?

Nothing made sense. She promised herself a long, hot

bath and an evening with a book. Apart from the party, there was nothing in her diary for tomorrow; she would find a suitable card and present for Mike.

Bradley Hinkston had stopped off in Plymouth as arranged but the house clearance sale had been a waste of time. He had left halfway through the bidding which he had watched just as a matter of interest. When he arrived home he was not surprised to learn that someone from the Avon police was coming later to ask him some questions.

Jack had arranged this and he remained at Camborne until the transcript of that interview was faxed through. Every few minutes he was tempted to pick up the phone and ring Rose but he knew it was best to leave it until he went home.

He studied the fax. It corresponded with what Rose had said almost verbatim, except she had omitted the threats Martin had made to Hinkston. Her loyalty had never been in question; she would not have wanted Dorothy's son to be under the slightest suspicion. It did, however, show that Martin was capable of threatening behaviour, although this was hardly unusual if he was protecting his mother's property.

The will surprised him. The lawyer in question had been more co-operative than some and Jack had been allowed to read the contents in the privacy of the older man's office.

Peter Pengelly was to inherit the house. 'It won't fetch a great deal,' the solicitor had told Jack. 'Its isolation will only appeal to a few, there's no central heating or double-glazing and it needs an awful lot of work done to the interior. A new kitchen and bathroom for a start.'

Even so it was a house with a saleable value and Jack would not have turned his nose up at it. What was interesting was that Dorothy Pengelly had left the remainder of her estate to Martin. This would include the house contents and her not inconsiderable savings which had now come to light. Why, then, had she been trying to sell off Martin's inheritance? Had she been worried that Peter and Gwen would get their hands on her valuables and sell them off or did she believe that Martin would not realise their worth and be duped out of them?

He studied the list again. It contained over thirty items. Alongside each was a detailed description and an approximate valuation. Jack whistled through his teeth. The amount in question made Martin Pengelly an extremely wealthy man and was motive enough for anyone to commit murder. Martin Pengelly would be as rich as a lottery winner.

Only one thing was wrong: the cheque Bradley Hinkston claimed he had given Dorothy for the Stanhope Forbes had not been paid into either of her accounts.

The bank had a record of a telephone call from Dorothy but the cheque had not, as Hinkston believed, been subjected to special clearance. Dorothy had only gone as far as to verify that there were enough funds to meet it. Therefore, he concluded, she at least had had it in her possession at some time. Had Hinkston somehow retrieved it? Surely he wouldn't have bothered writing it out if he had intended harming her.

And what of Martin? Had he killed his mother for the money because he couldn't wait for her to die? Did money actually mean anything to him? He drank too much but otherwise his needs were basic.

Jack shook his head in frustration. The timing didn't fit. Hinkston had visited Dorothy on the Thursday morning. Dorothy had had enough time to contact the bank and although an exact time of death was impossible to pinpoint she certainly had not died that early in the day. There was no reason for Hinkston to have waited, to have gone back later – he could have done whatever he intended whilst he was there. Unless, Jack thought, Dorothy had said she was expecting someone. Maybe Hinkston thought she would not have had a chance to pay the cheque in, which now seemed likely. With the man's consent they were now checking Hinkston's account to see if the relevant sum had been debited or transferred elsewhere.

He was too tired to think straight and Rose kept intruding upon his deliberations. He had not seen her cry before and, if he had his way, he would never let her do so again. But with Rose Trevelyan it was not a case of having his own way. He picked up the telephone and dialled her number. There was no reply but he had already steeled himself to that probability.

CHAPTER NINE

Rose woke at a quarter past four. The previous evening she had unplugged the telephone and enjoyed a long soak in the bath followed by a decent meal. At nine o'clock she had collapsed into bed and fallen asleep immediately, her unopened library book sliding off the bed unnoticed. Consequently she was awake early.

She opened her eyes and listened for sounds. There were none, not even the soughing of the wind in the chimney breast. Not a noise, but a dream, she thought, realising what had woken her. But it was rapidly dissolving, slipping away from her as easily as the sun burnt off an early morning mist. She tried not to think about it, hoping it would come back, but whatever pleasant memories it had evoked had now disappeared.

She padded downstairs, barefoot, and made a pot of tea. To her side were some notes she scribbled down; her own thoughts which could in no way be construed as evidence or facts. She studied them until the yellow light of dawn appeared on the horizon then decided to complete the work she had begun yesterday. She was rapidly approaching her goal but the jobs still on hand would be done to the best of her ability. Her own dissatisfaction, she thought, was nothing compared with that of Gwen Pengelly. Hooking her hair behind her ears she wondered what had made her think that. The downward turn of the mouth, maybe, the nervous energy? Or was it guilt? Still in her towelling robe she mounted some photographs under the enlarger. It was only six thirty. Ahead of her was a whole new day and she was going to take a walk along the beach. Rose, like almost everyone in Newlyn, knew the movements of the tide as well as most people know the days of the week.

As daylight rose into the eastern sky she stepped down on to the pebbles below Newlyn Green. All the rocks beyond the shore were exposed, dark and jagged against the limpid sea. There was no one in sight, which surprised her for she was not alone in taking early morning strolls. She wanted to speak to Doreen Clarke who would not have thanked her for a call before 7 a.m., even if she was an early riser.

Her shoes scrunched into the shifting mounds of stones until she reached the hard, wet sand left uncovered by the tide. She stood quietly, watching the waders as they fed along the shoreline and in the crevices of rocks. Most of them had returned now for the winter. A crow, unintimidated, scavenged alongside herring-gulls, dunlins sank their beaks into the yielding wetness and a flock of sanderlings scurried along the edge of the lapping water like miniature roadrunners. A man approached and let his dog off the lead. In unison the birds took off and circled until they felt safe to land again. The air was full of their wings and their calls. The Labrador stopped to sniff at something then ran on further, barking gruffly at a row of gulls further along the tideline. They squawked indignantly, rose as one then settled down again as soon as the dog had passed.

Rose walked the full length of the beach until the walls of the Jubilee Pool were towering above her. It was closed for the winter but she was fond of the 1930s art deco construction and had been pleased when it had been restored for use.

The tide crept slowly in. There was no way now around the pool whose foundations were built out on to Battery Rocks. She mounted the slope which led up to the Promenade, stamped the sand from her shoes and retraced her steps on firmer ground.

Doreen Clarke usually left the house at eight thirty; if she walked quickly Rose would just have time to catch her before she set off for work. She could not understand how anyone could choose to earn a living cleaning other people's houses, especially on a Saturday morning. Facing her own housework was bad enough for Rose.

'Anything the matter, dear?' Doreen inquired, surprised to hear the hesitancy in Rose's voice.

'No, not really. But there's something I wanted to ask you. Fancy coming over for coffee later?'

'Suits me. You know I always love a bit of a chat with you. Besides, I can't get any sense from Cyril at the moment, he spends half his time guarding those blasted vegetables of his. Don't ask me why, he hardly ever wins a prize.'

Rose was smiling when she replaced the receiver. Doreen was a good soul and down to earth but it was easy to see why her husband spent a lot of his time in the garden or greenhouse. He had suffered the same fate as many others when Geever mine closed but he had taken up gardening and Rose often benefited from his gifts of produce.

Armed with her painting things she set off on foot again. Going down through the village, she stopped for a moment to watch the auctioneers in the market as they gabbled the prices for boxes of fish. After choosing a birthday card in the paper shop she carried on up the Coombe, worrying about whether her choice of gift for Mike was acceptable. The river, to her right, flowed steadily, bubbling over the stones and under the bridge and spreading around the stems of the giant rhubarb which flourished there. To her left the fish shops were preparing for the day ahead.

When the pavement ended she took the path between two rows of trees and tried to remember exactly where Barry had told her she could find Saw-wort. It was, apparently, common in the south-west but scattered elsewhere, preferring damp, grassy places with woods nearby. Having taken the precaution of checking in one of her reference books she knew what she was looking for. It was a thistle-like plant but without spines and flowered until October. I'll say one thing about this, she thought, my knowledge of natural history's increasing.

As always when she painted, time passed quickly. Only the altered angle of the sun told her how long she had been working.

Regretting she had not brought the car Rose began the walk home. Some fishermen she knew were heading for the pub. 'Absolutely not,' she told them, smiling, but with a firm shake of the head when they tried to persuade her to join them. There would be enough to drink later.

Taking her canvas bag up to the attic Rose paused on the way back down to look at her new outfit which was on a hanger hooked over the top of the bedroom door. Yes, she thought, it's definitely me.

Turning away she pulled open the bottom drawer of the wooden chest set against the wall opposite the window. With shaking hands she lifted out a flat, rectangular object wrapped in clean sacking. It was the oil painting she had started when David first became ill and which she had completed in the dark months after his death. It had not been out of the drawer since.

'My God.' She almost dropped it. Finishing it was a vague memory yet now she saw it she clearly recalled almost attacking the canvas with her brushes. The strokes were strong, the colours vivid.

She propped it on the chest and stood back. As if her circulation had been sluggish Rose suddenly felt the blood pulsing through her veins. 'Bloody hell, Rose Trevelyan, it's good.' And it was. It was exciting and real: the picture lived. Had that been the missing ingredient of her youthful attempts? Were pain and experience necessary to produce decent work? No, she rationalised, not always, but they are with me.

The idea had been to give it to Mike but now she hesitated. Only when she conceded that if the past was to be completely behind her she needed to make this final gesture did she go down to the kitchen and wrap it in tissue and sheets of shiny gold paper.

Doreen arrived at twelve, straight from her Saturday job and before going into Penzance to shop. 'Like I said, you can't have a proper chat with Cyril under your feet,' she complained although Cyril was rarely in the house.

She sat down heavily and placed her bag neatly on the floor beside her, surreptitiously studying Rose's face. 'You look different, somehow, if you don't mind me saying.'

'Do I?' It was typical of Doreen that she had noticed. Rose felt different; alive and full of an enthusiasm that even Dorothy's death could not dispel. Or maybe her death was partly responsible for it, having made Rose aware that life should not be wasted. 'Well, I'm going to a party tonight.' Explanation enough for Doreen who would not understand the complexities of Rose's mental metamorphosis, or her decision concerning Jack.

'Ooh, lovely. Where?'

'Blast.' The telephone was ringing, Rose regretted plugging it back in.

'Keep away from Dorothy's place. Understand?' The voice was gruff, unrecognisable. The line went dead before Rose could say she would not be intimidated by someone too cowardly to give his name. 'I will not give in,' she said. 'I will not.' She returned to the kitchen determined not to let Doreen see that anything was wrong. Had she been watched that day when she couldn't find Martin? Perhaps it was not imagination after all.

'How's Martin? Have you seen him recently?' Doreen asked as she spooned two sugars into her coffee and stirred it vigorously.

'I think he's beginning to come to terms with it.' Rose

162

hesitated. 'Doreen, what you were saying the other day, about Gwen and Peter, is there anything else you can tell me?' Rose wished she had listened more carefully at the time.

'Maybe. Hey, you're not trying to do your young man's work for him, are you?' There was a glimmer of amusement in her eyes and her round, red face lit up expectantly, but Rose did not answer.

'Well, if you want my advice, and I don't suppose you do, he's a decent enough bloke and if he's any sort of a detective he ought to realise what a good catch you are.'

Rose appreciated the flattery but realised that it was useless discussing Jack with Doreen, who was of the opinion that a woman should be grateful for any man she could get hold of then make it her duty to keep him.

'What were we saying, dear? Oh, Gwen. Well, let me think.' She leant forward, elbows on the table, and lowered her voice conspiratorially. Rose knew more coffee would be required.

Jobber Hicks had taken it upon himself to become Martin's mentor. Dorothy was gone and the boy needed someone and, of all the people in the world, the two of them would never forget her. When he used to visit Dorothy, Martin was often absent or, if he did appear, soon took himself back up over the hill. Of course, in later years he had taken to living in the van and Jobber had seen even less of him. Star had settled down quite quickly but she, like Jobber, was getting on a bit. He felt there ought to be more he could do for the son of the woman he had loved. Yes, he thought, I did love her. It was the first time he had verbalised his feelings. Before, he had described her to himself as a fine woman, a strong one, and the only one he had wanted to marry. Perhaps if he had expressed his feelings rather than merely pointing out the benefits of their getting married things might have turned out differently. It was time to make amends.

The more he thought about it the more certain he became that his idea was a good one. The outcome would depend on Martin but he intended asking him if he would like to bring the van down to the farm. Jobber could find work for him, something manual, something which would not confuse or intimidate him. George could move into the farmhouse if Martin didn't want him in the van and they could, if Martin was willing, share some of their evening meals together. It would be company for them both. He did not want to admit that he wanted someone he could talk to about Dorothy.

Jobber had made up his mind but he was afraid to ask in case the answer was no.

Mike and Barbara Phillips lived in a rambling house out near Drift Reservoir. The facade was shielded from the narrow road by a hedge of evergreen shrubs but few cars or people ever passed the place.

Rose got out of the taxi and walked towards the front door, which was open. Light flooded from the house, spilling on to the uneven path and turning the leaves of the hydrangea beneath the windows a purplish blue. Its flowers had turned from pink to green and many were already dry and browning. The sound of music and conversation and clinking glasses made her realise how much she had been missing. She was just about to ring the bell when Barbara appeared in the doorway, chic in a straight silvery dress which would have made most people look shapeless. Her blonde hair was wound into a complicated chignon.

'Rose! Wonderful to see you. Have you come alone?' Barbara peered down the path before kissing her. 'Good. I'm glad.' She stepped back. 'My, my, you look great. What have you done to yourself?'

'Oh, it's the new clothes.' Rose smiled. There was a light in her eyes which had not been there for some time. She felt good in the muslin skirt with its black satin lining which caressed her bare legs as she walked. Tucked into it was an emerald silk blouson. Her auburn hair lay in soft waves around her shoulders and there were gold hoops in her ears, gold sandals on her feet. Under her arm was her gift.

She followed Barbara into the lounge which was softly lit. More than twenty people had arrived before her. Rose recognised several faces and, during the short journey across the room, was introduced to several more. 'Ah, here's the birthday boy.' Barbara laid a possessive hand on Mike's arm. Of medium build and with short brown hair and glasses, he was not good-looking but there was an air of gentleness about him and a kind curve to his mouth. He, too, kissed Rose and said how pleased he was to see her.

'About Dorothy – I'm really sorry.'

'It's all right.' Rose did not want to spoil the mood of the evening. 'Here, this is for you.' She handed him the parcel. 'Happy birthday.'

Mike turned to find a space in which to unwrap it. Placing it on a small side table he carefully removed the shiny paper and pulled away the tissue then he stood back. 'Oh, Rose,' he whispered. 'Oh, Rose, I never knew. Look, Barbara.'

Barbara came to his side and frowned before straightening up. 'Did you do this?' Rose nodded. 'Stella, come over here a minute,' Barbara called, waving an impatient hand to a black-haired woman in the corner. 'And you, Daniel.'

The couple approached them but no introductions were made until the painting had been examined.

Within three or four minutes Rose knew that her life had changed. Stella Jackson, whose own work was highly rated and who was rarely without an exhibition somewhere, expressed her genuine admiration, as did Daniel Wright, who was her husband and a sculptor. Daniel whistled through his teeth. 'It's terrific, Rose. Have you always painted?'

'Yes, but not like that.'

No one commented because they suspected what had happened – that Rose, like many artists, had become side-tracked along the way.

Stella was rounding up others to view the work. 'Are there any more?' she finally asked when Mike went to find a safe place for it.

'Not yet.'

Stella nodded. 'When there are, come and see me.' She wrote down her telephone number, then grinned. 'Come and see me anyway. We're in St Ives.'

'I know.' It was Rose's turn to smile at the woman's modesty.

'We'll have coffee, or something stronger. Now, let me introduce you to Nick Pascoe.'

The evening passed so quickly that Rose couldn't understand why people were beginning to leave. Glancing at her watch she saw it was after one thirty and rang for a taxi. Despite the wine she felt sober and clear-headed although she over-tipped the driver in her euphoria. It was hard to recall that it had been Mike's celebration rather than her own, but that was what it had felt like.

She ignored the messages on the answering machine and got into bed, not really wanting to take off her new clothes and spoil the magic of the evening.

Fred Meecham survived the weekend although he could not recall what he had done during the few hours that the shop had been closed. The world had become an alien place, or else he was an alien in it.

Monday arrived, bringing rain which swept depressingly across the harbour. It gurgled along the guttering and ran down the drainpipes noisily; appropriate weather for a funeral. In retrospect he could not recall attending one where it hadn't been raining, with the congregation huddled beneath dark umbrellas and the church smelling of damp wool. Or perhaps it just seemed that way.

He could not face the drive. It would have seemed disrespectful to turn up in the delivery van but he didn't accept any of the many offers of a lift. For the first time in years Fred organised himself a taxi.

He was numb, physically and mentally, but beneath that numbness lay fear and guilt. How wrong he had been to assume that the two deaths would close a chapter of his life. Other agencies were at work, dangerous ones. Rose Trevelyan for one, and Gwen Pengelly for another. Gwen with her avarice and her dislike of her mother-in-law, Gwen with her ambition and her pushy ways who would stop at nothing to lay her hands on Dorothy's money. And he had heard rumours about Martin, that the police wanted to question him again because he had easy access to the house and all that was within it. Why couldn't people believe that Dorothy had just decided to end her life? Dorothy had acted strangely on his last visit. Furtively was the word which came to mind. Someone had been there ahead of him, that much he guessed by the two cups and saucers on the draining-board. Dorothy only ever offered him a mug. Things were going on which Fred didn't understand and had no chance of understanding until Marigold was laid to rest and the sedative the doctor had given him had worn off.

The taxi driver was local and therefore made no attempt at conversation. What could he say to a man who was about to bury his sister, one to whom he had been exceptionally devoted? His passenger sat in the back which also precluded the opportunity to hold a proper conversation. He accepted the fare and the tip with a nod and a thank you and asked if Fred wanted collecting.

'No. I . . .' Fred shrugged. It didn't seem to matter what happened afterwards. He walked up the path towards the church. Organ music floated through the open doorway. He was almost overcome by the number of people standing around outside, nearly all of whom were his customers. Tears pricked behind his eyes. The cards of condolence had been one thing, this was overwhelming.

He nodded to acquaintances who stood back to let him pass as he entered the church. He sat in the front pew to which he was directed, his hands between his knees, quietly waiting. Most of the mourners remained outside, some of them enjoying a last-minute cigarette as if they thought it might be their last. Fred understood what such occasions did to people and he did not blame them. He dreaded the finality of the ceremony ahead but at the same time wished it to be over. As far as he could tell none of Marigold's relatives were present. There was no reason for them to be, it would have been strange if they had known. Out of the corner of his eye he saw Gwen Pengelly. He did not like her and he almost asked her to leave but a scene would be unthinkable.

As one the congregation turned when the organ music changed and they were asked to stand. At the back of the church was Rose Trevelyan.

Jack had telephoned on Sunday morning but Rose's cool tone discouraged him from making the conversation more personal. The Pengellys, Bradley Hinkston and anyone else, she said, were now his concern. Mentioning the party and the new acquaintances she had made, Rose hoped that she had thrown out enough hints for him to realise that the affair was coming to an end. All that remained was for her to see him face to face and tell him so but she despised herself for postponing it.

Her clean sweep as far as work was concerned was almost complete. Rose decided to emulate Doreen and clean the house before starting on the garden and the shed. Many of the summer flowers needed tidying and the grass required cutting. The final task, getting rid of the junk that had accumulated over the years, would be a painful pleasure. She knew there were still some of David's things in the shed but there was also a lot of rubbish. Once it was empty Rose would paint there. There were windows in the front and side, filthy now, but they could soon be washed, and they overlooked the bay. If she could succeed a second time, as she had with the one simply entitled 'Storm' which she had given to Mike, she would venture further for scenery.

Tired and grimy with soil and dust and cobwebs, Rose longed for a shower and a large gin and tonic. She had just undressed when the telephone rang. If it was Jack she would tell him there and then. The female voice was unfamiliar but Gwen Pengelly had kept to her word. She had rung to give the details of Dorothy's funeral. 'It's on Wednesday. Two fifteen at Truro Crematorium.' Rose did not ask the outcome of the inquest when Gwen said that the body had been released for burial.

'Thank you for letting me know.' She replaced the receiver and stood looking at it for several seconds. For Dorothy's sake she hoped there would be more than the direct family and one or two friends in attendance. Two funerals in one week, she thought sadly. Tomorrow Marigold was to be buried. Because Dorothy would have gone had she been alive, Rose decided to go in her stead. It was the least she could do.

In the shower Rose washed her hair and soaped herself twice but dirt was ingrained in the skin around her nails. Wrapped in her robe, her hair still wet, she sat in the window with a drink thinking of landscapes she wanted to paint. It was a peaceful evening and Rose enjoyed her own company. When she saw the black clouds building up in the night sky it seemed one might be directly above her. Remembering the telephone calls had shattered her tranquillity.

Because of the downpour dawn was a long time coming. Newlyn was a blur through the wetness. The forecast promised more of the same. There were no appointments for that day and there would be fewer and fewer if her new venture succeeded.

There was nothing black in Rose's wardrobe. After David's funeral she had vowed not to wear the colour again. She chose a brown suit and matching shoes, which hardly seemed to matter as whatever she wore would be covered by a raincoat.

Seated at the back of the church she concentrated on the other mourners. Gwen Pengelly was there, which was surprising.

When the service was over and Marigold's body had been committed to the ground she stood alone, half hidden by a tree, watching the vicar move from group to group and exchange a few words with each. Fred Meecham, she concluded, was going through the motions. Numbness allowed him to accept handshakes and whatever words of comfort he was being offered. The disbelief and misery in his eyes moved her. Rose trod carefully across the slippery grass and touched him lightly on the arm. 'Mr Meecham, I'm Rose Trevelyan. I met you a couple of times at Dorothy's house.'

She waited, puzzled at his odd expression, as if recognition was slow in coming yet she knew he had seen her earlier. 'Oh, yes. Yes, I remember. Thank you for coming.' Fred did not question her reasons for doing so. Rose put his peculiar manner down to despair.

'I'm so sorry. You'll miss her dreadfully.'

Fred nodded slowly. 'You don't know how much. I loved her,' he added forcefully, glaring at Rose. 'I loved her from the moment I first saw her.' He bit his lip. 'I – oh, please excuse me, everyone seems to be leaving. Are you coming back to the hotel?'

'Thank you, but no.' Rose would be an intruder amongst the people who had known Marigold better.

Fred nodded again, looking relieved that she had refused. Just in time she stopped herself from mentioning Dorothy's funeral. Under other circumstances Fred would have wanted to be there but she doubted he would be able to face it this week. She patted his arm once more as she turned to walk away then wished she hadn't when he flinched.

For several minutes Rose sat behind the wheel of the car and waited as people drove off. The rain had started again, becoming heavier until it was beating a tattoo on the roof. Fred's words came back to her again and by the time she had realised their possible implication the windows had misted over. 'I loved her from the moment I first saw her,' he had said. Of course, Marigold was a good deal younger than Fred: it could be that he, as an older brother, had loved her from the minute she was born. But Rose did not think so, and she was also beginning to believe that Doreen's idle gossip may have contained a grain of truth.

Many siblings, after death or divorce, lived with one another. Fred's wife had deserted him long ago and, according to Doreen, the same thing had happened to Marigold. 'But

I wonder?' Rose muttered as she turned the ignition key and thankfully heard the engine splutter into life. Instead of going home she turned left when she reached the main road and pointed the Mini in the direction of Truro.

'You've got to tell him, Rose.'

'Why should I? It's only guesswork.'

'Come off it, you wouldn't have told me if you really believed that.' Laura pushed back her dark curls which were hanging loose about her shoulders. They were sitting in Laura's living-room in front of the log effect gas fire. Rose had gone there upon returning from Truro. Outside it was almost dark although it was not much after six o'clock. Staccato bursts of squally rain hit the windows.

Laura had known that Rose was going to Marigold's funeral as well as to Dorothy's and she had been worried that too many reminders might be harmful so she had insisted that Rose came over for a meal and some wine afterwards. They were sipping a good claret and the effects of that and the warmth from the fire were relaxing. But Rose was not in the least depressed, if anything she was animated.

'I could have been mistaken. Doreen could have been mistaken.'

'You'll come to a bad end, as my mother was fond of telling me. Oh, wait a minute, I get it. It's not that you don't think it's important, it's because you don't want Jack to know what you're up to. Am I right?'

Rose's face was hot. Laura was a little too perceptive. 'Jack doesn't come into things any more.'

'But you haven't told him yet.'

'No.'

There was silence as Laura digested this information. 'All right, let's leave Jack out of it. What makes you think it's anything to do with Dorothy Pengelly?'

Rose sighed. 'I'm not saying it is, it's just that I feel there's some connection. Something which ought to be obvious but I'm buggered if I can see it.' She wanted to change the subject and wished she had not brought it up in the first place. But Laura was her friend, the one person in whom she could confide completely. All she had been able to discover were negatives but to Rose's mind that proved something because there were far too many of them to be pure coincidence.

'I'll see to the food, it should be almost ready,' Laura said, glancing at Rose and seeing that she was in a world of her own.

Rose was thinking about Fred Meecham. He had been born in Truro. Dorothy had told her that and Doreen Clarke had been able to supply the details of which street he had lived in. Fred was a churchman and never missed a Sunday service, logical then to make inquiries at the church nearest to Fred's old address. It had taken no more than twenty minutes to go through the parish register and find Fred's christening recorded. Both his parents had been buried in the churchyard. Marigold was younger man Fred so she used his dates as a starting point, working forwards from there. Marigold's name did not appear. Rose went back over the entries and checked the name Heath. Marigold had not been married there either. The incumbent vicar was unable to supply any information because he was new to the district.

Three times Rose checked the register but there was no

entry for Marigold Meecham or Marigold Heath. She had thanked the vicar and complimented him on his place of worship then returned to Newlyn and Laura's house.

Either Marigold had not been christened or Fred was being economical with the truth when he said that she had spent the whole of her life in Truro until she had moved in with him. But so what? And is it any of my business anyway? she asked herself. Then why had Doreen said, 'If they're related, then I'm the Queen of England.' The expression had made Rose smile. Someone less queen-like than Doreen was hard to imagine. 'You've only got to look at them, no way're they brother and sister. Now listen to this,' she had continued, 'and don't forget, I never repeat nothing 'less I'm pretty sure of my facts.' This had given Rose cause to hide another smile.

'Come on, Rose, let's eat.'

Laura's comment pierced her concentration. Rose got up and followed her to the kitchen where steaming bowls of fish stew and crusty bread awaited them.

Rose picked up a spoon and studied her face in the back of it. 'Everything's changing, Laura.' And as they ate Rose began to tell her what she intended doing with her life.

'And about time. Your watercolours are good, but you're capable of a damn sight better.'

Rose stared at her. This was the reaction from all her friends. Why had it taken her so long to discover it for herself? She grinned. 'This fish is delicious. But, Laura, dear, the service is a little slapdash this evening. My glass is empty.'

'Fill it up yourself, Mrs Trevelyan. You're not usually so coy.'

Once the dishes were stacked in the sink Laura fetched a second bottle of wine. 'I wouldn't want to risk being called inhospitable,' she said, waving it in the air.

Feeling that she had bored Laura with talk of Dorothy, Rose changed the subject. But just as she was leaving she couldn't help saying, 'Laura, I've been getting some odd phone calls.'

'Oh?' Laura's eyes narrowed. 'You mean threatening ones, don't you? And you haven't told Jack.' Rose shook her head. 'You must. Apart from any danger, don't you see that it proves there's something to hide?'

'Jack knows that. He's come round to my way of thinking.'

'You've always been the same, too bloody stubborn for your own good. Tell him, Rose, for goodness' sake.'

Ignoring the advice she continued, 'If you wanted to find someone, someone who had disappeared, how would you go about it?'

'Ask someone who knows them.'

'I can't do that. Besides, I don't want anyone to know what I'm doing.'

'Is this some sort of parlour game? No, don't tell me. And you can't ask Jack, of course. I don't know what's got into you, Rose. Perhaps Dorothy Pengelly is really a royal Russian exile and that Fred's sister, Marigold, was Mata Hari. Oh, God, I'm sorry, Rose, I know how much you cared for Dorothy. Forgive me, put it down to the vino. But please, please be careful.'

'It's okay.' Rose kissed her on the cheek. In a way the comment was no more than she deserved. She was inclined to get carried away. 'Ah, I must go.' They had both heard the toot of the taxi as it pulled up outside.

Rose's journey home was no more than half a mile but she did not want a soaking before she went to bed. She would not allow herself to admit how much the telephone calls had scared her. Thanking Laura for the meal she left.

CHAPTER TEN

Martin Pengelly told Jobber Hicks he would think about his offer. He could not bear the idea of leaving the only place that had ever been his home until after his mother was buried. He was not unrealistic enough to imagine the house would always be there for him, nor did he want to live in it alone. Having overheard enough of Peter and Gwen's conversations he knew that if it was up to them they would get rid of it at the first opportunity. At least his mother had been able to live her life out there. He still went to see to the cats and to feed George but he had not contemplated what would happen or how he would feel when someone else finally moved in. Peter would have to see to the paperwork and the will, Martin knew it was beyond his capabilities. The legal world was as much a mystery to him as technology would be to Star.

He did not know that Peter had been looking for him or that the police wanted to speak to him again. Most of his waking hours he spent tramping over the countryside that he had come to think of as his own. Jobber had found him, but Jobber always knew where to look. Only when it rained would he return to the van, soaked to the skin, and towel dry his longish hair. His body grew even firmer with the extra exercise but he was trying to walk off feelings he was ill equipped to deal with. He had not suffered pain like this before because Dorothy had always protected him. And now Jobber's idea was making him reel. It seemed too good to be true. He would have someone to talk to and he would see George and Star every day. What frightened him was that he was not used to being treated as normal. He could not understand why Jobber should want him around.

Martin no longer cried but the awful ache somewhere inside him wouldn't go away. He had no idea that Peter was also suffering, because his brother had never shown any interest in their mother. Gwen, he knew, disliked her intensely. At school Peter had run ahead or lagged behind when she came to meet them yet seeing her at the school gates had been the highlight of Martin's day. He had been very upset when Dorothy said they were old enough to catch the bus by themselves.

The tightness around his chest sometimes threatened to suffocate him, making him want to lash out. He knew the dangers of that so kept himself away from people. He had come very close to hitting Mr Hinkston the day he had found him snooping around but was glad now that he hadn't. When they met him in the pub he found he quite liked him. And Mrs Trevelyan thought he was all right, so he must be.

He trudged across the open land and the fields, mile after mile, until George was so tired he had to carry him. Suddenly he stiffened. In the distance, way down below him, he saw Gwen's car in his mother's driveway. Starting to run, he felt the panic subside. It was all right, she didn't have a key. He crouched beside a boulder and watched and waited. Gwen came away from the front door and walked around the side. Had he locked the kitchen door? Yes, he must have done. A few minutes later Gwen got back into the car. He heard the reverberation of the slamming door before she drove away. Martin did not know what to do but the one person who might be able to help him was Mrs Trevelyan. Although she was a lot younger and prettier than his mother she reminded him of her, and her house, although smaller, had the same feel about it. When she'd taken him there it seemed right sitting in her kitchen, not saying much, but letting go of some of the grief which the welcoming atmosphere seemed to absorb.

Bypassing the caravan he took George back to the house and opened some food for him. George ate half-heartedly then scrabbled at the armchair where Dorothy had once sat, managing to make it into the sagging seat on his third attempt. He fell asleep immediately. Martin watched him then gave him a gentle pat. He checked there was water in his bowl then went to the telephone and found the book with Rose's number in it. He dialled the digits slowly and carefully as his mother had taught him because he became confused if he got a wrong number. With relief he heard Rose's voice and not a recording of it.

As he listened to her calmly saying it was fine for him to come and see her any time he wanted, some of the tightness in his chest slackened. Tired from his long walk Martin knew he would have to catch the bus. One passed hourly along the main road on its way back from Truro. It would take him to Penzance bus station. From there he would walk the rest of the way. He had a handful of change ready and waited at the bottom of the drive. Despite the circumstances of his one and only visit to it Martin recalled exactly how to find the house in Newlyn.

Rose lay in bed for several minutes. Would she be able to paint before the mystery of Dorothy's death had been solved? She bit her lip and brushed the hair out of her eyes. Instinct told her to continue, that she was close to something even if she had no idea what.

Dorothy had left a will, which Martin knew about and, unbelievably, so did Bradley Hinkson. Bradley met Martin by chance, learnt of the Stanhope Forbes and then it disappeared. No, to be fair, Rose recalled, Bradley said he still had it and admitted leaving a print in its place as per Dorothy's instructions.

Marigold Heath was dead, although there was nothing suspicious in those circumstances, only sadness. She had been ill for a long time and everyone had known the only possible outcome, everyone except Fred who would not admit it; Fred who admitted that he loved her. But Fred had also known Dorothy, had spoken to her about the possibility of getting hold of a substantial sum of money for treatment for Marigold. Rose dared not continue with that line of thought, and she did not have a single fact to substantiate any of it. To mention her suspicions to anyone would be foolhardy and irresponsible and possibly cause irreparable damage to an innocent person. She had formed a hypothesis which was probably wildly off the mark. But to continue would be satisfying – except that she needed a copy of a birth certificate and without a name, date and place of birth, and other details such as the father's occupation, she would not be able to procure it. Only one thing was out of place. Why, in this day and age, would anyone care? That was the question which had revolved in her subconscious all night.

Now it seemed she might have the answer. Fred Meecham was a church-going man, he lived the life of a good citizen nothing was too much trouble if he could help someone out. Too good to be true? Rose wondered. Or did he have something to hide? Yet it still seemed impossible to imagine that Fred had killed Dorothy because she would not give him the necessary funds to send Marigold to America. Rose was very much afraid she was fitting the circumstances around the facts rather than the other way around.

Dorothy had hinted that there was more to Fred than met the eye. And there was something else, some hint, some small clue, something which might mean nothing. 'I tried to talk him out of it, I said he should spend time with Marigold, not waste it seeking the impossible.' Dorothy had told Rose how she tried to convince him of the wildness of his scheme. Had Fred then helped himself to Dorothy's painting and, noticing the switch, had she called him to task and had he then killed her? Too far-fetched, Rose, she told herself, and how would he know it was there? As far as Rose was aware few people had known. But what about that envelope? Had she misread what she took to be Dorothy's way of telling her something? Stop it, she told herself. This isn't getting you anywhere.

An aunt, Dorothy's last surviving relative apart from her sons, had left her the money. The proceeds had come from the husband's business, coffee, she thought it was, somewhere in Africa when times had been good. That was no longer important. Laura was wrong, Rose thought, I don't believe Marigold Heath was Mata Hari but I don't believe she was Fred's sister either. She was trying to rationalise something that was no more than a gut feeling and she hoped it was not simply a way of avoiding facing Dorothy's death in the way she had done with David's. Tell Jack, her conscience kept saying. Sod him, her emotions retaliated. Her better nature dictated that matters should be left alone but curiosity and stubbornness were not so easily conquered.

Rose had half a dozen photographic assignments left to fulfil and she would not let her customers down. Soon she would be mixing with artists again; she was impatient, but she did not want to give up one area of her life leaving a bad taste behind. One of the messages which had been waiting on her machine was an invitation to dinner at Stella and Daniel's place in St Ives on Sunday. There would be eight of them.

Rose wondered who had been invited to partner her.

Piling her equipment into the car she suddenly knew what her next move would be. She returned home just in time to take Martin's call.

A knock at the front door an hour and a half later puzzled Rose because she wasn't expecting anyone and most people came around to the side. 'Martin!' she exclaimed when she saw him standing on the doorstep, his face sorrowful. She was astonished that he had taken her up on her offer so quickly. 'Come on in.'

He followed her, pleased that they were going to the kitchen and not to some other room. There was a pile of clothes in a basket on the table waiting to be ironed and a strong smell of coffee. Martin only drank tea but he thought he wouldn't mind trying whatever it was Mrs Trevelyan had in the machine that spluttered and hissed.

Rose followed his eyes, smiled, and got out two mugs. She offered him milk and sugar, moved the clothes basket to the floor and sat down with him. Martin was not the sort to pay a social visit but he seemed reluctant to break the silence. 'Is something the matter, Martin?'

Martin pushed back his thick hair and nodded. 'I don't feel right. I hurt and nothing looks the same any more. Am I sick?'

Rose's own emotions were in turmoil as he described what he was feeling. 'No, you're not sick. It's what happens to people when they lose someone they love. It'll pass, Martin, I promise you it will. But it takes time, sometimes a very long time. Have you told Peter any of this?'

'No. I ain't seen 'im. Nor 'er, not till today. She was snooping up at the house. And now I don't know what to do.'

'About what?' Gwen, up at the house? She would think about that later. She listened as he explained about Jobber's proposal and once more she felt a great warmth towards the man who was prepared to step in and take over where Dorothy had left off. At the same time she was disgusted with Peter for ignoring his brother. 'I don't want to be there when there's new people.'

'Is the house being sold?'

'It'll have to be.'

'Is Peter seeing to all that?'

184

'I dunno. But I don't know if 'e knows about Mother's papers. I don't think she told 'un where they was. She told me, though.' He folded his arms across his broad chest as if to underline the importance of what he was saying.

Rose frowned. She had told Jack where the will was, surely someone should have contacted Peter and Martin by now. But perhaps someone had and that was why Peter was keeping out of his brother's way. If only she knew what was in it.

'I wasn't to tell, see, about the papers.'

Rose understood. The will had been a secret between Martin and Dorothy but he realised it was time his brother knew although he was not prepared to tell him himself. 'It's all right, the police know all about it. I had to tell them, Martin.'

He surprised her by smiling. 'I knew you'd do the right thing. I never thought of that.'

'Would you like some more coffee?'

'Yes, please. 'Tis lovely.'

As she poured it Rose recalled the tension between Peter and Gwen and wondered again what might have been the cause of it. 'Would you like me to speak to your brother?' She had uttered the words before she had a chance to think of the wisdom of them. Whatever the response, it was Martin she was thinking of. He nodded enthusiastically.

The telephone conversation was brief and to the point. Rose was sure that Peter knew of the existence of a will by now but it would put Martin's mind at rest.

'Dorothy's solicitor has been in touch,' Gwen Pengelly said coldly. 'Not that I think it's any concern of yours.'

'It isn't,' Rose replied mildly, 'but Martin wasn't sure if you knew.'

'Martin! Oh, I suppose he was told first.'

Rose mumbled something and said goodbye. Gwen could think what she liked, at least some unpleasantness had been avoided. What infuriated her was that no mention had been made of Martin, no inquiry as to how he was or even where he was. Rose walked stiffly back to the kitchen trying not to let her anger show. She explained to Martin what would happen now but that these things took time. There was nothing he need do, the solicitor would see to it all. 'You might have to go and sign some papers but if you like, I'll come with you.' Satisfied that he understood and saw there was nothing to fear she gently broached the subject of his mother's funeral and offered him a lift to the crematorium. That was something else which seemed not to have crossed Gwen's mind, how he would get there or even if he knew when the ceremony was taking place. It had been Jobber who told him, who had gone to the trouble of ringing up to find out when the service was to take place. 'Look, why don't we do as we did before? You go to the farm and I'll pick you and Jobber up at the same time. I'll ring him to let him know.'

'Like the other night?' He seemed to take comfort in the fact that the three of them would be together.

'Yes, something like that. Now, shall I run you home?' But Martin would only take a lift as far as the bus station. He showed her his return ticket so Rose let it go at that. 'Hang on, I'd better make that call first.' She did not want Martin turning up at Jobber's only to find he'd got a lift with someone else or taken his old pick-up truck. 'That was lucky, he'd just popped in before seeing to the hens.'

'Don't you keep no pets?' Martin looked around the kitchen for evidence of one.

'No. Not since I was a child.'

Martin thought about this. 'You ought to. Where's your husband then?'

For a split second the pain came back. 'He died, Martin.'

'Like Mother.' There was another pause. 'So we're the same, you and me. You ought to get yourself a pet though. I'll tell 'e what, you can have one of the cats if you want.'

Rose smiled, touched by the kind offer, but she did not have the heart to say that there was no way she would give one of Dorothy's cats house room. 'Thank you. But I'm used to being on my own and I go out a lot. It wouldn't be fair. They're happier out in the country.'

As they drove down to the station Rose chatted casually about the following day, wanting to make sure Martin understood exactly what was to take place.

'Mr Meecham might be there,' he said. 'He used to come up and talk to Mother. He's got someone dead as well. Marigold.' Martin gave a small giggle. 'Silly name. Mother always reckoned she weren't his sister. Why would he say she was if it weren't true? Seems daft to me.' His face was flushed. He was unused to making conversation and felt he might have said too much. Nothing Dorothy told him was ever repeated but it was somehow all right to tell Mrs Trevelyan.

'She told you that?' Rose took her eyes briefly from the road.

''Ezz, course she did. Who else would tell me? Mother always talked to me, I reckon she thought I wasn't listening half the time. She knew lots of things, did Mother. She knew Marigold wasn't no Cornishwoman.'

'She wasn't?'

'No. Couldn't understand it myself. I knew Mr Hinkston wasn't from round these parts, 'twas obvious, but I wouldn't have known about Marigold. Mother did. She said to me, "if that's not a Plymouth accent, I don't know what is".' He nodded several times, pleased with his fairly accurate mimicry of Dorothy's voice.

Plymouth. The accent was a lot different, just as local accents varied in different parts of Cornwall. If Dorothy had spotted it then others must have done too. Was that what Doreen Clarke had alluded to? 'Are you sure?'

'Course I'm sure. Mother was never wrong. She said it weren't broad because Marigold had picked up the way we do talk, but she knew, Mother knew.'

All thoughts of forgetting her theory were wiped out. This new information gave her something to work on. But surely it would be impractical, if not impossible to go searching in Plymouth. Or would it? A perusal of the telephone directory for Heaths could do no harm, it covered the whole of Cornwall and Plymouth. If that failed it really would be the end of it.

Rose made a quick calculation. Marigold had been younger than Rose and both Rose's parents were still alive, which reminded her she must ring them. It had been over a week since she had last done so. She smiled as she thought of their busy lives. Unlike many of their contemporaries retirement had not made them less active. They treated it as an opportunity to do all the things they previously did not have time for and they were rarely to be found at home. So far they had both been spared the inconvenience of the infirmities of the elderly and she hoped it would remain that way. They were close, but not in a cloying way. After David died they had done all they could before returning home. It was Laura who had threatened to get them back down if Rose didn't start living again. For a long time they had insisted upon a daily telephone call, made by one of her parents each evening. Four Christmases they had given up to be with her. Until the last one. Then they had taken a cruise, happy in the knowledge that Rose was to be spending the day with Jack Pearce.

There was a strong smell of kelp in the air as they reached the Promenade. A wind had picked up and was drying the brown weed where it lay in heaped piles along the beach, washed up by the high tides.

She saw Martin on to the bus then went home. There was a lot to think about, including Gwen's visit to Dorothy's house, and she wondered if she had been gullible in taking Bradley Hinkston at face value. Wasn't he a little too urbane, too sure of himself? And what ready replies he had had to all their questions.

DI Jack Pearce had done all he could and was becoming more and more convinced that he was wasting time on a matter which did not merit it. Roy Phelps had now also been questioned by the Avon police.

Jack ran through Phelps's statement once more. Both

he and Hinkston claimed the former had not been near the Pengelly premises. More than likely this was true otherwise Phelps could have been used to alibi Hinkston. Once, or if, the cheque came to light then the picture might be a little clearer.

Halfway through the morning he received a call from Dorothy's bank manager. 'I only became aware of it today,' he told Jack, 'but Mrs Pengelly had a meeting with our financial adviser on Thursday afternoon. It was arranged rather hurriedly but he managed to squeeze her in. Apparently she was in the process of setting up a trust fund for her younger son, Martin, using the cheque you were inquiring about. We have a copy of the forms with her signature on but the papers from the trustees won't yet have reached her address. Mr Rowe, that's our financial adviser, is here with me now if you want a word with him.'

Jack did, but he only received confirmation of what he had just been told. Mr Rowe, he thought after the call was over. It was a common enough name in Cornwall but it still had the power to disrupt a good mood. He believed Rose when she said there was only friendship between herself and Barry, but what Jack envied was the long-standing relationship, the years which the two of them had had to get to know one another. He was, he supposed, plain jealous but he could not expect her to stop seeing Barry. At least he had the answer to the missing cheque, but why Dorothy Pengelly had gone about things in such an unusual manner was beyond him. Surely people set up trust funds when their children were small? Then he began to understand. To make the necessary arrangements had meant selling off her valuables. Dorothy had probably wanted to enjoy them for as long as she could and only as she reached what soon would naturally have been the end of her life did she decide to provide for Martin in this way. Martin would not be able to handle a large sum of money, nor would he have known how to go about selling the house contents. Even if he had done so there was the danger of his brother, or his brother's wife, persuading or cheating him out of his inheritance. This way Martin was guaranteed an income that could not be misused by himself or Peter. Another point crossed Jack's mind. Rose had said that Dorothy was concerned about the amount of alcohol Martin sometimes consumed. A regular income would prevent him blowing the money on drink in a few years whilst ensuring her son's needs were met for the rest of his life. Another motive out of the window.

So what next? As he ran a hand through his dark hair Jack realised it needed cutting. Too often lately the job seemed to come before all other things, especially Rose. Not that she complained. Not that she seems to care at all, he added silently but bitterly. 'What next is that I forget the whole thing.' The words were addressed to the empty room in which he was sitting. Hinkston and Phelps were surely in the clear; Dorothy Pengelly's death might have been untimely but it no longer seemed suspicious.

It was after six before he got the chance to ring Rose. His stomach knotted with disappointment when he heard the click of the answering machine. He was missing her more than he liked to admit. He was about to leave a message when he heard what he thought sounded like 'Oh, bugger' over the top of the recording. Then 'Hold on.' He smiled as he pictured Rose running down the stairs to answer the call but getting there too late. The line cleared. 'Hello?'

'Hello, it's me.'

'Ah, Jack.' There was a pause. 'I'm sorry about that, I forgot the stupid thing was still on.'

'How are you?'

'I'm fine.'

There were times when he wanted to shake her. She sounded so offhand and not in the least pleased to hear from him. He could not recall knowing a more infuriating female. 'Are you free tonight?'

'Actually, I was going to ask you the same thing. You see, there's something I need to talk to you about.'

'Oh?'

'Not on the phone. Can I meet you somewhere?'

'Yes,' he said as his stomach churned. 'Wherever you like.'

Somewhere quiet, Rose thought, somewhere where we won't come across any of the numerous people we know between us. But in West Penwith that was almost impossible. In the end she decided on the Cutty Sark in Marazion. Jack agreed to be there at eight. Whatever happened he would not be late.

Later, under the shower, he felt as though his life was on the line. Unlike Rose he did not possess intuition or what was often referred to as a sixth sense, but that evening Jack would have bet money on what she was going to tell him.

Rose was nervous, unable to think of the best way of breaking the news. There is no best way, she decided, I'll have to take it as it comes. Beneath her anxiety was the anticipation of the dinner with Stella and Daniel and the knowledge of her next move as far as Dorothy was concerned. I still have the keys, she thought, but she was reluctant to use them. It had to be more than coincidence that after each visit to the house she had received an anonymous call. Someone was watching the place. Her pulse raced. Or me, she amended.

But crowning everything was the sight of the canvas, primed and ready for her to start work.

At seven thirty she went out to the car. It was a balmy evening, the wind had dropped and the sky was clear. It would not be too long before the clocks went back and the rhythms of winter were set in motion.

Because she was early, Rose left the car in the car park some way down the road from the pub and strolled, hands in the pockets of her jacket, up towards it. People were eating at the polished wood tables at the front of the premises but over their heads she saw Jack standing against the bar which ran at right angles to the door. She swallowed.

'Dry white wine?' he asked, his voice carefully neutral.

'Please. With soda.'

Having paid for the drinks Jack turned to face her. 'Well, Rose?' Towering over her all he could see was the top of her head because she was studying the contents of her glass.

She sighed, shoulders drooping, before she met his eye. 'Jack, I'm sorry. I'd like us to be friends but . . .'

'I see. So it was just a fling.' His voice was like ice.

'No, it wasn't that, it was much more than that.' She felt near to tears seeing the pain and bitterness in his face. 'I'll never forget what you've done for me. You see, after David

I thought there'd never be anyone else. And then I met you and you proved me wrong.'

Jack nodded slowly. 'Yes, I see. I was the trial run, the practice before you got back into the swing of things. Thank you so much for telling me.' He threw back his drink, emptying the glass. 'Well, sod you, Rose Trevelyan.'

'Jack, wait, I'm scared.' Rose spoke quietly but it was too late. His glass was on the bar and there was an empty space beside her. Briefly his large frame filled the doorway and then he was gone, a few heads turning inquisitively to follow his departure.

Rose smiled stiffly at the barmaid who could not have helped but overhear their conversation then she finished her drink, taking her time because she did not want anyone to see how upset she was.

As she drove back to Newlyn a few spots of rain hit the windscreen but she would be home before it started in earnest. Jack, she thought, would no longer bother about Dorothy Pengelly. All the time she had believed he had taken an interest only because she, Rose, was involved. Suicide. And why not? Except, through her own foolishness, she had not told Jack about the phone calls. Laura was right, they proved there was more to it than that. It's up to me now, she thought, standing in the space between the parked car and the kitchen door. Heedless of the rain she was unwilling to enter the house just yet. She inhaled deeply. The air smelt different. There was the usual salt tang and the rich smell of damp earth but there was something else. Rose realised it was the scent of freedom.

* * *

Marigold was at peace. Fred, with the assistance of some of his customers, had had to organise drinks and sandwiches in the function room of a hotel in Hayle. He would not have bothered but the two women who came to help serve in the shop had been shocked and told him it was expected. It was ironical to be paying for the sort of food he could have provided from the shop but he had had no intention of inviting people back to the flat.

The day after the funeral he felt exhausted, as if he had been awake for many more nights, but sleep eluded him.

Tomorrow was Dorothy's funeral but he would not be attending. It was too soon after Marigold's for it to mean anything.

With a jolt he realised the relevance of this. His face, which for so long had been creased with misery, altered. What he had started had been a waste of time. It didn't matter now. Whatever Dorothy had in the house didn't matter, no one could possibly find out now. The knowledge should have brought comfort but as the hours passed it had the opposite effect. He required certain knowledge and he wouldn't rest until he had it.

CHAPTER ELEVEN

Rose, too, tossed and turned. She felt bad about Jack but her life was changing. Ever since she had arrived home from Marazion she had been expecting him to ring. He had not. Perhaps he remembered it was Dorothy's funeral the next day and thought better of causing an argument.

Her body heavy with lack of sleep she dragged herself out of bed in the morning. What she was about to do was against her better judgement but for Dorothy's sake she would do it.

Half an hour before she was due to pick up Martin and Jobber she pulled up outside Dorothy's front door and let herself into the house. Standing still she listened. She was alone and there had been no sign of life outside. Holding her breath she opened the drawer beside the sink in the kitchen. There was the envelope she had seen Dorothy place there. She picked it up. It was sealed and her own name, in Dorothy's spindly writing, was on the front. 'Well, well,' Rose said as she slipped it into her handbag. There was no time to think about it now.

Martin was waiting anxiously at the end of the lane when

Rose's Mini came into sight. He knew what to expect but he could not have faced it alone. The anger was still there, burning away inside him, but Jobber had said that that was all right, that soon it would go. He was very glad that Mrs Trevelyan would be with them, nothing could go wrong. The only other funeral he had attended had been that of his father but he was too young to remember anything other man the sun which had beaten down on his uncovered head and the solemnness of the adults which had seemed out of place on such a lovely day.

Rose saw Martin standing apprehensively in the gateway. It seemed impossible that it was only yesterday afternoon he had come to her house with all that had intervened. She had returned from dropping him at the bus station and gone straight up to the attic to attend to some paperwork, forgetting to switch the answering machine off. When she ran down to intercept the call which she had hoped would be from one of her new acquaintances it had been Jack. As soon as she had heard his voice she had known that the time for procrastination was over. There had been no word from him since.

Rose waved and tried to smile, putting herself in Martin's position. 'It'll be all right, you'll see,' she told him as she got out to let him into the back seat. 'Where's Jobber?'

'He's just coming.'

Rose got back behind the wheel. Without anyone suggesting it Martin had dressed in grey trousers, a white shirt and a tie. She had no idea where the tie had come from but guessed it was an old one of Jobber's. Over this he wore a waxed jacket which was the only coat he possessed. The sky was a clear blue but a cold wind blew from the east. Rose suddenly realised that the weather was irrelevant, Dorothy was being cremated, they would not be out in the open.

'Ah, here he is.'

Jobber walked down from the farmhouse towards them, his bent legs working quickly. He, too, was dressed in his best clothes, in his case a dark suit, shiny with age. Rose was surprised to notice the black tie and armband. She did not realise that people still wore them.

'Morning,' he said solemnly.

'Hello, Jobber,' she replied as he got into the front passenger seat. She did not know which of the two men looked the more despondent. 'Shall we go?' It was an inane question, only intended to break the tension but no one answered.

At first they thought that Dorothy's funeral had attracted a crowd until they realised that the mourners milling around were from the previous service and had gathered to look at the flowers which were laid out for inspection. Their own party consisted of the three of them, Peter and Gwen, and two elderly strangers Rose did not know. There was no sign of Dorothy's grandchildren. At the last minute Doreen Clarke hustled into one of the pews, her face red beneath her tea-cosy hat. 'I managed to get an hour off,' she whispered as the music stopped playing.

"Tis a sad day,' Jobber said, wiping his eyes when they filed out. 'Are you all right, boy?'

Martin nodded. He seemed stunned.

After the short service Peter came over to them and thanked them for coming then, after a noticeable hesitation, invited them back to the house. Rose did not know what to say. She had provided the transport, if she drove Jobber and Martin back to Hayle who would take them home? It was Peter's duty to see to it but she doubted if he would.

Jobber met Rose's eyes and gave a small shake of the head before he looked at Martin. 'Do 'e want to go back to your brother's?'

'Of course he does,' Gwen said, taking his arm.

'No. I'm going along with Mrs Trevelyan.'

'Are you sure?' Rose asked, noticing the disparaging look Gwen gave her, as if she alone was responsible for Martin's decision. Peter showed little interest in the interchange. There were dark shadows under his eyes and his skin seemed to be sagging. He stared into the distance somewhere above their heads. Gwen's attitude was entirely different. She seemed brisk and efficient, trying to organise people, but Rose noticed she was trembling and unable to meet anyone's eye.

In the car Rose suggested that they ought to do something in the way of seeing Dorothy off. She invited Jobber and Martin back to her cottage.

'Naw. 'Tis out of the way, girl. You both come back to me. I've got a drop to drink and Angela's there with the kiddie, she can soon knock some sandwiches together.'

Rose had not been inside the farmhouse before. It was warm and comfortable and not a bit as she had imagined it to be from the outside. The furnishings were shabby but it was a home, one which was loved and lived in. Star was livelier than she had ever seen her. She got out of her basket clumsily and licked Jobber's and Martin's hands. George growled, which made Rose smile. Something was as it should be. The

Jack Russell had been adopted into farming life in advance, Rose suspected, of Martin's joining them.

'I heard they was wanting to talk to Mrs Pengelly again,' Jobber commented innocently as he poured three glasses of port. 'They say 'er car was seen up at your mother's place the same day as she died.' The words were addressed to Martin but Rose knew they were meant for her. She supposed by 'they', Jobber meant the police but she had no idea how he came by the information. That was one of the quirks about Cornwall, everyone seemed to know everything without actually being told. It was as if knowledge was absorbed by osmosis. But this piece of information did not fit in with the picture she was building up. Was she so wrong, was it Gwen Pengelly who was watching her?

Rose stayed for only half an hour. The port was strong and she had to get the car home and catch up with some work. Martin was having supper with Jobber so she knew he would be in safe hands for what was probably the worst day of his life.

Once home Rose felt the sudden need of someone to talk to. She rang Barry. 'Are you busy?'

'No. Hardly anyone about today, surprising as it's turned out fine. Mind, it's bloody cold in the wind. And you know I'm never too busy for you, Rosie.'

How she wished that Barry would not make his feelings so obvious. He was bound to gloat when he heard about Jack.

'How did it go this morning?'

'As well as these things can. There were only a few of us there.'

'I think you need a bit of cheering up. Look, let me take you out tonight. Put your glad-rags on and we'll go and have a decent meal somewhere.' And please don't say you've already arranged to meet Jack, he prayed.

'I'd love that. Thank you, Barry.' They arranged a time and she hung up, picturing him in his white shirt, the sleeves rolled up as he worked his way through the ever-increasing mound of paperwork which littered his desk in the back office. He reminded her at times of an absent-minded professor. Perhaps it was the thick-rimmed tortoiseshell glasses which did it. He's a good friend to have, she thought, as she settled down to some paperwork of her own.

Barry's main downfall was the lack of a sense of humour. He took life and himself too seriously, which was the opposite of what Jack had accused her of. But that evening he excelled himself. Sensing Rose's grief over Dorothy and something else he was unable to define, Barry went out of his way to entertain her and he managed to succeed.

'So, what plans for the immediate future?' he asked as he helped her on with her coat prior to taking her home.

'I'm having a shopping trip to Plymouth. It's ages since I've done that.'

Barry knew Rose's aversion to shopping but refrained from commenting. Perhaps Jack was taking her out for the day which might make it more appealing. He did not want to know. When she changed the subject he decided he was wrong, that Rose was probably off on one of her crusades, and he wanted to know even less about that. Of course, it might all be innocent; Rose rarely bought new clothes but perhaps the trip was intended to cheer herself up after losing

201

a friend. At least he could credit himself with having helped a little in that direction.

Neither of them mentioned Jack. Rose knew that to make a point of explaining the situation would only lead Barry to build up his hopes. She thanked him for the meal and left him wondering what was going through her mind.

Thursday morning dawned crisp and bright. Too crisp for September. Rose shivered as she pulled her dressing-gown around her waist and belted it tightly before closing the bedroom window. Twisting a towelling band around her hair she went downstairs.

In the garden the leaves were beginning to show signs of red and gold. Autumn was usually late in Cornwall, but not that year. The climate, despite the rainfall, was suitable for subtropical plants to flourish. Rose could only ever recall one occasion where frost had damaged them.

While the water trickled through the coffee machine she fingered the envelope which still lay on the table. Addressed to herself it contained no letter, only a street map. A few days ago it would have meant nothing, now it told her that her suspicions were correct. That Dorothy had left her a message, cryptic though it might be.

Plymouth, she thought, as she gazed out upon the now tidy garden. There were plenty of trains and there was no point in going through an endurance test with the car. She checked her timetable and picked an early one. Penzance being the terminus there would be plenty of seats. Half an hour later she set off on foot, enjoying the level walk along the Promenade and the crisp wind in her hair.

She bought a day return ticket and a coffee to drink on the train. For the first half hour she looked out of the window, emptying her mind of all that had gone before that week. The sea was rolling in over the sands of Marazion beach. Shallow breakers with white crests broke along the shore. The causeway leading out to the Mount was still covered. Later, when the tide turned, people would be able to walk across.

Rose had made sure her credit card and cheque book were in her handbag. Whatever else happened that day she was determined to buy some more new clothes. But before she did that she was having coffee with Audrey Heath.

The simplicity with which she had found Marigold's mother had been astonishing. Her number had been listed in the telephone directory, although it was not the first Heath she had rung. She was not certain who Mrs Heath believed her to be. Rose had been vague over the telephone and allowed her to draw her own conclusions. Having ascertained that she was related to Marigold Heath, and Rose did not think there could be two people of that name, she had said she wanted to ask her some questions. Mrs Heath had said she would be pleased to talk about her daughter but, in her own way, had been as enigmatic as Rose.

The train pulled into Bodmin Parkway before Rose realised where they were. It would not be long now. Mrs Heath lived in St Budeaux, on the outskirts of Plymouth, but the Inter-City train on which Rose was travelling passed through the small station there without stopping. This meant catching a local train or getting a taxi as she was uncertain of the bus routes.

Loud tannoy announcements greeted Rose as she stepped on to the platform. Hurrying across the brightly lit concourse she had to swerve to avoid passengers gazing up at the arrival and departure screens. Outside a row of black cabs stood waiting. The driver of the front one was reading a paper but he reached out of the window and behind him to open the door without looking up as if he had sensed Rose's arrival. She gave him the address and folded herself into the back seat. The driver chatted as he negotiated the city traffic. She was only half listening because they were driving down streets she did not know and she was curious, taking everything in.

Soon she was knocking nervously on Mrs Heath's front door. The house was identical to the others which lined the road. Muffled footsteps were followed by the sound of a bolt being drawn. A round face peered out through a gap of a few inches before the door was opened fully. 'Mrs Trevelyan? You found me all right then?'

'Yes.'

'Come on in. I didn't know what to think when you rang, but if it's to do with Marigold, well, I thought it was time I knew.' The Devonshire vowels were rounded, the speech slower and more drawn out than Rose was used to hearing. She did not have a good ear for accents but the difference was obvious. If Marigold had retained a trace of her origins then Dorothy would not have missed it.

She followed Mrs Heath down a narrow hallway, the carpet of which was protected by a clear plastic runner. There was to be no formality, she was shown into the kitchen. It was clean but untidy. A bottle of milk stood on the table alongside a plate of toast crumbs. Mrs Heath made no excuses nor did she remove the plate. 'I more or less live out here. It's warmer in the winter and I get a better reception on the telly. Take a seat. I'll put the kettle on then we can have a chat.'

Audrey Heath tipped the used tea-bags from the pot into the sink. As the kettle boiled she lit a cigarette and offered Rose the packet. Rose accepted one, it was the brand she smoked. It was a useful prop, something with which to occupy herself as she thought how best to approach the subject. It was quite clear that her hostess did not know her daughter was dead.

Rose noticed that beneath the shapeless grey skirt and pink sweater Mrs Heath wore elasticated stockings. Her feet were swollen and a small roll of flesh hung over the sides of her slippers. Rose was unable to put an age to her, she might have been anywhere between early sixties and mid-seventies. This, then, was Marigold's mother to whom Rose had to break the news. She did not think she could possibly leave without doing so.

'Sugar?'

'Sorry? Oh, no thanks, I've got sweeteners.' Rose dug into her bag to get them out, still unsure what to say.

'It's nice having a bit of company. I don't get out much, with my legs, you see. Where did you say you were from? My memory's not what it was.'

'Newlyn.'

'Down Penzance way. That's a fair old way to come.' Audrey looked pleased, as if the length of the journey was more important than what her visitor had come to talk about.

Rose knew she had to make a start. 'Mrs Heath, as I explained, the questions I want to ask are for my own interest only, nothing will go any further without your permission. I'm not from the press, or anything like that.' She paused, thinking what a mess she was making of it. Perhaps, from the strange way in which she was being observed, Mrs Heath may have been expecting payment or to hear good news. Stalling was useless and she could not continue until the truth came out.

Audrey nodded. 'Whatever you say can't hurt me, dear. I've got nothing to hide.' She sipped her tea noisily, the cup held in both hands because her joints were gnarled with arthritis.

'I don't know how to put this. There's no easy way. Mrs Heath, it's bad news, I'm afraid.'

'Concerning Marigold.' The statement was flat. 'I can't say it surprises me.'

Audrey's reaction was nonchalant and therefore unexpected. For a minute Rose thought there might be another Marigold Heath. She had to make sure before she continued. 'When did you last see your daughter?'

Audrey squinted through the smoke. 'Some years ago now. Not since she left home.'

'Where did she go?'

'Where she was destined to go. Downhill. Oh, don't look so upset, that girl was trouble from the minute she was born. By the time she was sixteen she was on the game, nothing I could do to stop her, she never took a blind bit of notice of me. I suppose it's true what they say, about kids needing a father. Hers was killed when she was small. She used to

206

pick up seamen, did Marigold. There's enough of them in Plymouth. Sometimes down Union Street, sometimes down the Barbican, but that was before they done it all up. It's real nice now. Next thing I heard was that she'd taken off for Cornwall. Not even a goodbye. Don't ask me why, she didn't know anyone down there. Still, we were never what you could call close, not really. Marigold always kept her distance, even as a little girl.'

Rose swallowed. It felt painful. 'Mrs Heath—'

'Oh, Audrey, please.'

'Audrey, Marigold died last week.'

'Died?'

'Yes. I'm so sorry. And I wish there was someone closer to you who could have broken the news.' Rose half stood, ready to put a comforting arm around her shoulders. It was not necessary.

'I always said she'd come to a bad end. Someone strangle her, did they? Wouldn't surprise me, I was tempted to myself many a time.' She paused and stared at Rose. 'No. Can't be that, the police would've come round.'

The words were harsh but there was no other way to put it. 'She was ill. Marigold died of cancer.'

'Oh!' Audrey's face registered a mixture of emotions. Shock and pain and regret but no grief. That would come later. 'I wouldn't have wished that on her, no matter what she did.'

'I went to her funeral. I naturally assumed all the family knew, I can't think why someone didn't tell you.'

'It was very kind of you. Thank you. But I don't think I'd've gone if I had known. We fell out badly and she said she never wanted to set eyes on me again. I'm glad there was someone like you there to say goodbye.'

'There were an awful lot of people, over a hundred.'

'What?' Audrey's eyes bulged in disbelief, then she laughed. 'Maybe all her clients turned up. How was she, I mean did she do all right for herself?'

Rose saw Audrey reach into her pocket for a tissue and make a pretence of blowing her nose. 'Yes. She did all right. Did she have any brothers or sisters?'

'No, she was the only one. I couldn't have coped with two like that.'

Rose was safe to carry on. 'Marigold had a boyfriend. They were together for some years. They ran a shop and from what I know she was happy enough. She didn't want for anything and her boyfriend adored her.'

'Marigold turned respectable? My God. Running a shop, you say? I never thought I'd live to hear such a thing.' Audrey sighed deeply. 'I wish she'd let me know, I wish she could've just telephoned me. Perhaps she was afraid I'd tell this bloke about her past, but I wouldn't have, I wouldn't have said a word.'

Rose saw that it was a double loss. First her daughter had walked out on her then she had lived the sort of life Audrey would have wished for her.

'Were there any children?' She held her breath.

'No.' At least she had not missed out on that.

The tears still held at bay, she asked Rose to talk about her, to tell what Marigold was like.

'I didn't know her, but I met the man she lived with. He was quiet and, as you said, respectable, a church-goer,

208

a warden, I believe. They had the shop and until Marigold became ill they both worked there. She was well liked by the customers.'

Audrey was shaking her head as if Rose was talking about someone else. 'She wasn't a bit like that at home. I tried everything I could think of to keep her on the straight and narrow, but by the time she was fourteen I knew I was wasting my time. Then just before she left the police wanted to see her. Something to do with a man who was stabbed in the street. Three o'clock in the morning, it was. Of course, she wasn't here, she'd left home ages before that. Turns out he was her pimp. No great loss to the world to my mind. All the girls were questioned and once they knew he was dead they were more than willing to speak. I don't condone the way they earned their living but I did feel sorry for them knowing how he treated them. Marigold had been seen with him that night – mind you, she'd been seen with other men too. Not long after that she went away. I heard they were satisfied that she wasn't involved after some man came forward and said how he'd spent the whole night with her. She didn't come home, not even then. Later I heard she'd moved to Truro.'

'Why there?'

'Beats me. Another city, maybe, although not so big as this one.' Audrey pushed back a lock of hair. It was grey except at the front where nicotine had stained it yellow. 'I always wondered if she'd taken up with one of her men, one of the ones that used to come up here to get what they weren't getting at home, if you see what I mean.'

Coincidence? Rose did not think so. Fred Meecham

originally came from Truro but he already had the shop when Marigold moved in with him. She may have said that Truro was where she was heading but it was not where she had ended up.

As for Fred, that was the part which puzzled her. He made such a big thing of acting the perfect citizen and of being deeply religious. Had he really come to Plymouth to visit prostitutes? And could a girl like Marigold have changed so drastically? Or had it been what she had wanted all along, a man and a life of domesticity? They would never know now. 'What happened in the end, about the man who was stabbed?'

'Oh, I don't remember now. You know how it is, big news one minute and the next everyone's forgotten all about it. I can't recall hearing they got anyone, but good luck, I say, if it prevented other girls getting beaten up. Here, if this chap was so fond of Marigold, how come they didn't get married?'

Rose shrugged. 'I've no idea.' It was a good question. Both of them were single, perhaps Marigold did not want it. But why pose as brother and sister? Surely even someone like Fred would not be embarrassed in this day and age. There might have been gossip to begin with but, as Audrey had said, things soon blow over. Rose was certain there was an explanation which had nothing to do with the conventions.

They talked for a little while longer then Rose said she must leave. She felt she knew a great deal more about Marigold Heath now than she did about Fred Meecham. Audrey tried to persuade her to stay to lunch but Rose refused. She held out her hand. 'Thank you for seeing me, and I really am sorry.'

Audrey clutched her hand in both her own. 'You've nothing to be sorry for, dear. It's me that should thank you for coming. And it's easier now I know she found a man to care for her.' Audrey shut the door but Rose saw that as she did so she was pulling the tissue from the sleeve of her jumper.

There was a bus stop at the end of the road. Rose had given no thought as to how she was to get back to the city centre and there was no telephone box in sight from which to ring for a taxi. As she was deciding on the best course of action a young woman with a pushchair arrived at the stop. Rose asked her how to get back into the centre of Plymouth.

'There's a bus in a couple of minutes, it'll drop you in Royal Parade.'

Rose thanked her and smiled at the toddler who was smacking at the plastic hood protecting him from the wind. They were high up and Rose could see the gantries of the huge cranes in the dockyard. When the bus arrived she carried the pushchair on to it, leaving the mother's hands free to cope with the child and to pay for her fare.

Alighting in the city centre Rose crossed at the lights and studied the posters displayed inside the plate glass windows of the Theatre Royal. If she had thought about it in advance she could have booked a matinee seat but that wouldn't have left any time to buy herself something to wear. With her new-found freedom there were many things she could do.

Strolling through the pannier market she eyed the colourful stacks of fruit and vegetables, noted the cheapness of the meat and fingered the swinging bundles of pungent leather handbags. The mixture of aromas was almost exotic but over all was the warm, meaty smell of pasties, Devon pasties, with the crimped crust running along the top instead of around the edge.

Leaving the market she walked up New George Street towards the main shopping area. The wind off the sea, stronger now, gusted up Armada Way. In a department store she bought three sets of matching underwear but did not see a dress or suit she wanted.

Rose liked the spaciousness of the city, rebuilt after the heavy bombing of the war with its added attractions of the Hoe overlooking Plymouth Sound and the Barbican, steeped in history with its cobbled streets and eating places and art galleries and where she and David had once done the tour of the gin distillery. It was housed in a building which had been a monastery and a prison amongst other things. It was after three and she had almost given up. In desperation she went into a boutique from whose doors throbbed rock music. And there she found exactly what she was looking for; bright, flamboyant clothes, items which reminded her of her youth. But it was not her adolescence she was trying to recapture, it was the freedom of spirit she had once possessed. As she came out of the changing room a flowered dress caught her eye. She tried it on and bought that too. Her purchases wrapped and paid for, she left the shop.

With a smile of satisfaction she walked the last couple of hundred yards back to the station and was just in time to catch the London train, Inter-City.

It was dark when she arrived back in Penzance and there were damp patches on the pavement where a passing shower had occurred in her absence. Although she had walked a fair distance in Plymouth she needed to stretch her legs after the two-hour journey. As always, each time she returned she felt as though she had been away longer and it was a pleasure to fill her lungs with the fresh salty air.

She walked briskly, carrier bags swinging as she looked forward to a drink and a meal. She had not eaten anything since breakfast.

It had been an odd but enjoyable day. Rose was thinking about what Mrs Heath had told her but nagging at the back of her mind were Jobber's words, about Gwen Pengelly having been seen at Dorothy's place on the day of her death. Gwen was aware of her involvement with the family and must surely have been suspicious of her reasons for calling on her and Peter. That's it, she thought, remembering the details of the neat kitchen and the immaculate appearance of her hostess. Beside the kettle had been a brown plastic container of pills. Tranquillisers? Rose wondered. Gwen had struck her as the type of woman to resort to them. And if so? No, Jack would have made inquiries. It was not up to her to speak to the woman. Wrapped in thought she had not seen just ahead of her, leaning on the railings, a man whose profile, even outlined against the darkness, she recognised. Smoke trailed from a cigarette as he tapped ash over the sea wall. It was Jack. She was about to cross the road when he turned his head and saw her. It was too late to avoid him and it would have been childish to pretend she had not seen him. She carried on walking, more slowly now.

'Rose?'

'Hello, Jack.'

They stood looking at each other. 'Are you on your way home?'

'Yes.'

'I was just taking a walk. Rose, I've been out of my mind since I saw you. I wanted to ring you. Every minute I've wanted to but I told myself it was no good, you wouldn't speak to me. I owe you an apology, I was very rude. Are you still angry?'

'No, Jack, not angry. Disappointed, though, because I'd hoped you'd understand. Believe me, it wasn't your fault.'

He threw the end of the cigarette to the ground and stepped on it. 'I'd like to remain friends. I've had time to think about it and I promise you there'll be no pressure.'

She was ashamed to acknowledge a new disappointment. Jack Pearce seemed to have got over her very quickly. 'Good. I must get home, I've had a long day.' She swung the carriers. 'I've been up to Plymouth.' It would mean nothing to Jack. Marigold's death was not the one he was investigating but she felt a mean streak of smugness that she knew things of which he was completely unaware. Her white plastic bags glistened under the streetlights as she began to move away.

Jack's eyes moved over her face. Rose had enjoyed herself, he could see that. He would not have been able to if their roles were reversed, but there was something else, an undercurrent of excitement which had nothing to do with her day out or seeing him. 'Can I buy you a drink?' he asked quickly before she had taken more than a couple of steps.

She hesitated before agreeing. It would be a test, a way of seeing if Jack would keep to his word. 'Yes. But it'll have to be a quick one.'

214

He did not ask why, he was too pleased that she had not refused. They crossed over and walked back to the Yacht which was set back from the front, a Union Jack and the Cornish flag flying from its turreted roof. Like the Jubilee Pool, it had been built in the thirties.

Rose ordered a gin and tonic, Jack had a pint of beer. They took their drinks to the curved seat in the bay window.

'Have you eaten?'

'No. But I've got something planned at home,' Rose said firmly. Seeing Jack unexpectedly had unsettled her. There were things she knew now which she ought to tell him and things she had guessed at, but it would mean spending more than half an hour with him to discuss them and she was not ready to do that.

'Okay.' His tone was light and almost relaxed. Rose wondered if he thought he'd won a minor victory.

They spoke little, neither sure what would now offend the other. One thing was certain, the relationship was on a different basis. To emphasise this Rose told him about the party and the dinner to which she had been invited and then she said she must leave.

He nodded and stood as she picked up her bags but he was not going to make the mistake of offering to walk her home. Instead he went back to the bar.

Peter Pengelly had taken the rest of the week off. After the funeral he and Gwen had returned to the house with the two elderly friends of Dorothy's whom neither of them really knew but who, having participated in many such events, expected to be fed. Gwen had done her best to be charming but was relieved when they left. She was aware that their departure quickly followed a comment about collecting the children who had gone to a neighbour's straight from school.

Now it's over, she thought, now we can get on with our lives. She had cleared away the plates and glasses and thrown the paper serviettes in the bin. It would have been a mistake to discuss anything with Peter that evening. She knew he had struggled through the day, trying to be polite when all he had wanted was to be alone with his thoughts. Now, twenty-four hours later, he sat in his chair in the living-room facing the blank television screen. She had no idea what was going on in his head.

Gwen gave the children milk and biscuits although they would be having their tea soon. She was trying to silence them because they were noisily demanding to know what exactly had happened to their grandmother. She looked at them fondly. They and Peter were her life. Would there be enough to be able to afford to send them to private schools? But not as boarders, she couldn't bear that. Guilt did not tarnish her anticipation of the money that was to come although waves of it kept taking her unawares. With her back to the children she swallowed one of the tablets prescribed for her although they did little to reduce her permanent anxiety. No one could have seen her go to the house that day or the police would have questioned her about it. No one need ever know.

Shushing them once more she left the children at the table with instructions not to disturb their father. Rearranging her features into what she hoped was a semblance of sorrow she went to see what comfort she could offer Peter.

* * *

The shop was closed and had been for over an hour. Illuminated only by the streetlights Fred Meecham's face was pudgy and jaundiced. He did not know how long he had been standing there, only that his legs had stopped trembling, but they ached. He peered around in the gloom and pulled a plastic milk crate towards him, upended it and sat down, oblivious to the discomfort of its hard moulded surface.

All this was his. The shop, the goods, the living accommodation overhead. His kingdom, as he used to joke with Marigold. His kingdom, and she was the queen. She used to like it when he called her that. It might not be much by some people's standards but to Fred it represented a lifetime's work and loyalty to his customers which they had repaid. So many shopped at supermarkets these days. Now there was no one with whom to share it all and this saddened him. One day everything would go to his son who would sell up and it would be as if Fred Meecham had not existed.

It shouldn't be this way, he kept thinking. Marigold was so much younger than himself. He should have been the first to go, she would have been left in a comfortable position. Now he would have to change his will. He supposed he ought to do the right thing by Justin even if they did not communicate. Marigold had given him more happiness than he had believed possible although he had been aware that his love was not reciprocated in quite the same way. Until the end her feelings had been those of gratitude and fondness. That did not matter. Having her under his roof had been enough for Fred. The first time he met her on one of those shameful visits to Plymouth he had recognised a need in her, one that he believed he could fulfil. To the best of his knowledge he had done so. The security she had craved he had provided in the only way he knew how and he had removed her from danger, protected her to the end. He would continue to protect her for ever. His only regret was that they had not married, but they had been agreed upon that because it was too much of a risk. The bond that united them had been secrecy.

His life loomed ahead, stretching endlessly into nothingness, the days marked only by the opening or the closing of the shop. He jumped when he heard someone tapping on the window. Peering in, hand shading her eyes, was one of his regular customers. Wearily he got up to open the door. 'You couldn't let me have half a pound of butter, could you? I wouldn't have disturbed you, but I saw you there and, well . . .'

'It's no trouble.' The words came automatically, he used them almost every day of his life. He took the money and gave change from the float in the till. It made no difference how long the hours he worked, there was always someone who had run out of something. Knowing that in some small way he was needed, he had decided to keep on the shop. There seemed little point in selling, he had nothing else to do with his time.

He knelt on the cold floor and prayed. 'Forgive me, God,' he said. 'Forgive me. It was all for Marigold.'

Sometimes God answered him, Fred could hear His voice, but more and more lately there seemed to be no response.

He double-locked the shop door and went up to the empty flat.

* * *

As Martin walked past his mother's house he ran his fingers along the rough granite wall, almost enjoying the scrape of the stone in this farewell gesture. The sun was rising behind the hilltops but there was a low-lying mist in the valley above which everything else was crystal clear. Dew sparkled on the grass and stained the leather of Martin's boots as he breathed in the richness of damp vegetation. There was time to kill until Jobber came with his tractor to tow away the van. Everything was ready, Martin's few possessions were stowed away in the overhead lockers or firmly tied down. The previous afternoon they had made a thorough check of the vehicle because it had not been moved for many years. Jobber had seen to the tyres and inspected the tow-bar and between them they had made the necessary adjustments.

George had already gone to the farm, Jobber had come for him the day before Dorothy's funeral. There had been an ecstatic reunion between the two dogs until they each remembered their respective positions in life and settled down to ignore one another. The cats, too, had gone with him, spitting and scratching until Jobber had them safely in the back of his truck, the sliding glass windows firmly closed behind him as he drove for fear they would go for his scrawny neck. Back at the farm he had opened the rear doors and all three cats had fled screeching across the yard. Whilst they were seeing to the caravan Jobber had said they had disappeared, but he had found the remains of several rats and mice so he knew they could not be far away. They would be useful. His own cat, Mathilda, had never shown the slightest inclination to do what should have come naturally and Jobber had had to resort to poisons to keep vermin at bay. Mathilda preferred the comfort of the hearth, an armchair and regular supplies of food which she did not have to catch herself.

Jobber had thought it best to remove the animals first. It would be less of a wrench for Martin when the time came and they would be there at the farm to welcome him.

Martin stopped. A pane in the window of the back door was broken. It was no accident. The glass had been knocked out and the door was unlocked. Had George still been on the premises the intruder would not have got away lightly. His face paled. If it wasn't Peter or Gwen trying to get in without a key then it had to be Hinkston come back to get his mother's things. Hinkston knew that his mother was dead and that the house would be empty.

Carefully stepping over the shards of glass which glinted in the weak sunlight he went inside. Puzzled, he walked from room to room. Nothing seemed to be missing.

Martin was sitting on the step of the caravan when Jobber arrived. He was pleased to hear the noisy engine of the tractor as it made its lumbering progress up the side of the hill.

Jobber stepped down, nodding seriously when Martin told him what he had discovered. 'All right, boy, let's go over to the house and tell the police.' He had a good idea who might be responsible but kept his thoughts to himself.

Despite their preparations it took until the late afternoon before they were on the move. First they had to wait for the arrival of a patrol car then they had questions to answer. As nothing was reported as missing the two officers suggested it was a case of vandalism, kids who had heard that the place was uninhabited and who had probably been scared away by the hoot of an owl or headlights which played over the hillside as cars rounded the bend. DI Pearce had been making inquiries about the sudden death of Mrs Pengelly, so they decided to inform him of the vandalism, if that was what it was. It could be that someone had smashed the window in order to remove evidence or, if it was Martin himself, who held keys, in order to make it look that way. The police officers left them to it.

Just as they thought they were ready, one of the tyres went down and as they began their descent the sound of grating metal caused them to stop and investigate the underside of the van. Finally they were on the road and began the painstaking journey to the farm. Jobber was watching the road and the traffic coming from the rear, Martin sat sideways in the front of the tractor, looking over his shoulder, keeping an eye on the movements of the vehicle they were towing. Neither of them saw Peter's car as it headed towards Dorothy's house once more, this time in search of Martin to tell him about the appointment on Monday.

Gwen had received a telephone call from Dorothy's solicitor in Truro asking if she and Peter could go in and see him on Monday regarding the contents of her will. She agreed readily although she was not certain of Peter's shifts. Martin was to be there too although Henry Peachy had been unable to contact him. Gwen offered to let Martin know or to get Peter to do so. Silently she made plans for the future, their future. Hiding her excitement was not easy.

'The van's gone,' Peter said when he returned that

evening. Only as he said it did he realise that he had passed it. It was unremarkable, old-fashioned and painted cream, but he had not been expecting to see it being towed behind a tractor. It had not crossed his mind that Martin would ever go anywhere else. The first person he thought of was Jobber Hicks. He telephoned the farm and was surprised to learn that Martin had taken up residence there, then he waited until his brother came to the phone.

'He'll be there,' Peter told Gwen. 'He said he'll make his own way.'

Gwen nodded, hoping that Rose Trevelyan was not involved with Martin's transport arrangements.

The answering machine was blinking furiously as Rose opened the sitting-room door. Nine calls, she calculated, watching the flashing light in disbelief. But only three messages had been left. Jack's was the first, a tentative 'Rose? Are you there?' followed by a pause and the clunk of his receiver being replaced. The next came from Jobber who asked apologetically if she could ring back as soon as possible. 'You've let yourself in for it,' Rose told herself. The final message she replayed twice, forgetting the six non-existent calls.

'You may not remember me,' a smooth male voice said. 'My name's Nick Pascoe, we met at Mike and Barbara's. I wondered if we might meet again. I own a gallery just outside St Ives and I was impressed with your work. I was hoping there are some more like that.' The pause lasted for so many seconds that the first time she listened Rose thought he might have been cut off. 'Look, what I said is absolutely true, but

I'd like to see you anyway, Rose.' She grabbed a pencil to write down the number he was dictating slowly then she sat down to think about it.

Stella and Daniel had introduced her to Nick, who had said little at the time. She recalled the lanky man of an indeterminate age, dressed in jeans, a fisherman's shirt and a frayed denim jacket. His greying hair hung over his collar. But his face was what she remembered best. It was a strong face; uncompromising, lined, firm-featured and weathered, but his eyes were unreadable, the grey pupils speckled in a way she had not encountered before. In her excitement at meeting new people she had supposed he had taken little notice of her. She knew his work but she had not met him until that evening.

It was after nine and Rose had no way of knowing whether the number was that of the gallery or his home address but she refused to get out the phone book to check, nor would she appear too eager by ringing back at once. Just as she was deciding what an appropriate time might be, the phone rang again. She reached for it immediately thinking it might be Jack, that he had not accepted what she had said and was going to start pestering her. 'Hello?'

'I warned you. This time—'

'This time, nothing. You're wasting your time.' Rose slammed the receiver down so hard she thought the plastic might have cracked. Too late she realised how foolish she had been. She was alone in the cottage, unprotected, and she had not told Jack about the threats. And she could not, would not ring him now. He would misread the situation and think she had made it up just to get him over there.

Three times she had been to Dorothy's empty house, three times she had been threatened. And instead of keeping the caller talking, trying to recognise the voice or background sounds, she had hung up. Desperate to hear a friendly voice she rang Jobber.

'Dorothy's place's been broken into,' he said without preamble, 'but young Martin sez nothing's gone missing. We called the police and I've boarded up the window as best I can. Martin's here with us now. You don't think it's our fault, maid, do 'ee?'

'How can it be?' Rose sank into a chair. Bad news followed bad news lately. She had been up to the house herself, she might be in some sort of trouble. With a sickening feeling she knew that whoever had also been up there had been looking for what was now in her possession. But why? Why had Dorothy made such a thing of it? Why not just tell Rose and be done with it? Then she knew. It was typical of Dorothy. She wanted justice to be done but not at the cost of additional pain.

'That there Hinkston fellow, we told 'un Dorothy was dead. Martin thinks he came back to help hisself.'

'But you just said nothing was missing. Besides, I just can't see it.'

Jobber was silent. Rose imagined him scratching his grizzled head or rubbing his unevenly shaved chin.

'I 'spect you're right. Oh, there's something else.' Rose held her breath. 'Martin's got to go to Truro on Monday. Peter rang to say so.'

'About the will?'

'Tha's right.'

'And he wants me to go with him.' Well, she had offered, she couldn't back out now and he would need someone on his side.

'If it's not putting you out.'

'Of course not. What time?'

The arrangements made, Rose poured a stiff gin and tonic. Tomorrow, no matter what, she must face the situation. She could not live with threats and the danger was real, she knew that now.

That night, for the first time since she had lived there, Rose drew the curtains and shut out the view of the bay. Then she made sure every door and window was firmly locked. When she went to bed she left the downstairs hall light on in case anyone was watching. They might believe she was still up.

The enormity of what she had done hit her as she lay, wide awake, beneath the duvet. She had removed what might turn out to be a vital piece of evidence, even if it was addressed to herself. Tomorrow she would know for sure.

CHAPTER TWELVE

Dorothy Pengelly was very much on Jack's mind despite several other pressing cases. If Rose's premise was correct, and Dorothy had not taken her own life, then who had? It was peculiar dealing with something he could not put a name to. This was no clear-cut murder, it might not be murder at all. However, certain things did not fit. The paracetamol bottle Martin had explained away. His mother kept them for his use. Jack did not need an explanation, he assumed they were for the times when Martin had over-indulged, and although the bottle had been lost along the way it was not paracetamol which had caused Dorothy's death. Nor was it any of the drugs which Marigold had been prescribed: he had not just taken Meecham's word for it, he had checked with her GP, the same GP who prescribed the mild sedatives for Gwen Pengelly. And, as Rose had said, Dorothy herself was not on the list of any local doctors. So where had the Nardil come from? The pathologist had said it was not a common drug and rather old-fashioned now, though still useful in certain cases. Phenelzine was its proper name and

226

it was used in the treatment of depression and phobic states. More importantly it was an MAOI, which to Jack had meant nothing. 'Monoamine Oxidase Inhibitor. Risky to give to depressives because it reacts badly with certain foods and alcohol and it shouldn't be prescribed for the elderly.'

'So someone in their seventies who's never taken medication could swallow these MAOIs with alcohol and die.'

'You swallow enough of anything with alcohol and you're not going to be too healthy,' the pathologist had replied.

Fine. But who, if not Dorothy, had got hold of the stuff? And who had now broken into the place? They had been back once, with Martin who had let them in on the occasion when they had questioned him. There had been no sign of anything containing alcohol yet the PM results showed that Dorothy had been drinking. This alone was enough to convince Jack that Rose was right. Someone had been there and someone had removed the bottle. He had cursed himself for not realising this sooner but, on the other hand, there could still be another explanation. Dorothy may have accepted a drink knowing what was likely to happen, and whoever had provided it was innocent and had simply thrown the bottle away or taken it home with them because she had said she would not drink it. It didn't hang together, though, not when he thought about it. It was hardly likely that Dorothy, receiving a visitor bearing alcohol, had suddenly thought, I'll kill myself.

Who was the visitor? Who was it who had removed the bottle and washed up after them? Martin? Peter or Gwen? Rose? She was a welcome visitor and Jack knew that she had not been left out of the will. Jobber Hicks and Fred Meecham were her only other friends. Bradley Hinkston? The first transaction seemed genuine but had he gone back for another look or for some other reason beyond Jack's imagination?

Several times he had gone through the statements taken from those who had known Dorothy. He was not entirely happy with Gwen Pengelly's account and Rose had expressed suspicion of the woman. Now there was more evidence – if it could be so called, for it had been given anonymously and was, as yet, unsubstantiated. Gwen Pengelly had been seen at the house prior to the death. He must speak to Peter's wife again.

All the time he sat at his desk the telephone remained silent. Now and then he would glance at it as if he could will it to ring and Rose to be on the other end. He had left a feeble message on her machine.

Sighing, he picked up his jacket, felt for his car keys and drove over to see Gwen Pengelly.

She had worked it out, she was sure she knew what had happened to Dorothy. Once she had proof Rose was going to contact Nick Pascoe. When she met him she wanted nothing more on her mind than art and the pleasure of his company. It was as if she was keeping him as a reward for her efforts.

She needed someone to accompany her because of the risk involved and did not listen to common sense dictate that Jack was the answer. Was Barry or Laura more suitable? It was Barry's number she finally dialled, having stood by the phone chewing a nail for several minutes.

'But why?' he wanted to know, sounding surprised.

'If I told you you wouldn't come.'

'What on earth can I do with you, Rosie? All right, what time? Seven's fine. No, don't argue, if we're going, we're going in comfort. I'm not risking my neck in that bone-shaker of yours. I'll pick you up.'

'Thank you.' 'Thank you,' she whispered again as she stared at the phone. All she had to do now was to get through the rest of the day.

Nick Pascoe's words echoed in her mind. There were no more oils, not like the one she had given to Mike, only the immature attempts of her youth and the not very interesting ones she had painted after her marriage.

Rose went up to the attic and got out her easel. It was adorned with cobwebs; it was a very long time since it had been part of her equipment. At the back of the cupboard, carefully wrapped in clean sacking, were several canvases but she would need more. Having packed the one she had already prepared, plus the easel, paints and brushes, into the back of the car she went back into the kitchen and filled a flask with strong coffee. She pocketed an apple and a banana and set off. Could she execute another oil as good as the one she had given Mike Phillips? Yes, she kept telling herself, yes, you can. And all the time she was conscious of what she was going to do later and wondered what she was letting herself in for, how much danger she was in.

It was many months since she had been to St Agnes but the journey was worth the trouble. She had needed to get away to paint and to try to forget and the steep ruggedness of the landscape suited her mood. Surf rolled into the bay and covered the sand in long sweeps, and droplets of spray caught the sun like prisms. From where she sat on her canvas seat, partly sheltered by the bonnet of the Mini, the wind still took her breath away. She tied a scarf around her hair and pulled a heavy jumper on top of the one she was wearing, then she got down to work.

The sky was clear but it remained cold. Only when Rose's fingers were too numb to continue did she stand back from the easel which she had stabilised with metal pegs and study what she had achieved. Excitement flooded through her. The painting was nowhere near finished but she had blocked out the background and fixed the perspective and the initial brush strokes were confident. But it was more than that, she saw that she had painted with her emotions as well as with her skills. Instead of limiting her, fear and anger had set her free.

It was a pleasure to be out of the cold. Rose let the car engine warm up then began the drive home.

She said nothing to Barry about where she had been and why, that would come later, when the painting was finished. He was punctual, as she had known he would be.

'You're right, you know. I really ought to get out more often,' he said as they drove smoothly down through Newlyn, his car engine purring quietly, the padded seats comfortable behind their backs.

Rose glanced across at him. He sat with his head jutting forward, both hands on the wheel, as he peered through his glasses at the road ahead. For once they remained firmly on the bridge of his nose.

'Pull in here,' Rose said as they approached the car park of the pub where she and Martin and Jobber had met

Bradley Hinkston. 'I thought we'd have a drink first, we've got plenty of time.' She had told him that if he was prepared to accompany her she would treat him to a meal but there was something she had to do first.

There were other customers waiting to be served and not many spare seats. 'I know this is your treat, but you must let me buy you the first drink, by way of celebration.'

'Celebration?' It was the last thing on Rose's mind.

'Mm. Your new life?'

'I see. Thanks, I'll have a white wine, please. Look, you order it, I'm just going over the road. There's something I want from the shop. You'll be served by the time I get back.'

Half puzzled, half amused, Barry nodded and held out a five-pound note to attract the attention of the busy bar staff. The smell of the food wafted out from the kitchen at the back of the building and he began to feel hungry. He wondered where Rose was taking him, he was more man ready to eat. At last it was his turn to be served. He got the drinks and moved to the corner of the bar where there was more room.

Rose hurried from the pub, looked both ways and crossed the road. The tide was out and fishing-boats leant against the harbour walls, seemingly stuck in the mud and shadowy in the darkness. There were no other pedestrians in sight.

Fred Meecham's shop was open, as she had known it would be. Dorothy had told her that winter and summer he did not close until nine.

It was more than a grocery store. Apart from the shelves and cold cabinets stocked with food there was now a pile of wire baskets to enable customers to help themselves. There were the usual postcards and toiletries and a small rack of paperback books. At the back, in heaps, ready for the colder weather, were bags of coal and logs. In the spring their place was taken by bags of compost.

Rose swallowed, it was now or never, then she progressed slowly down the aisle to the far end of the elongated shop. Fixed to the wall was a slotted wooden box which held free pamphlets advertising local places of interest. She flipped through them idly. Fred was busy at the till serving a woman with a basket full of goods. When she left they were alone.

'Can I help you?'

Rose had not heard him approach but she was unaware he had been able to see her in the curved mirror which hung over the counter from where whoever was serving could watch for shoplifters. Her actions may have seemed suspicious for she had not taken a basket and did not seem to know what she wanted. She forced a smile. 'I've brought you something. From Dorothy. I think you were looking for it.' She reached into her shoulder bag, almost dropping it because she was trembling. As she looked up and met his eyes she knew with certainty that she was right. Dorothy had known but she had left it to Rose to do whatever she thought was necessary. When Marigold was dead, Rose realised. But had Dorothy had some sort of premonition that her own life would end prematurely?

Fred took the envelope she held out to him, glanced briefly at her name on the front of it then withdrew the street plan of Plymouth. He froze when he unfolded it and saw the cross, marked in red felt-tipped pen at the corner of two converging streets.

Whatever reaction she had been expecting, Rose was totally unprepared for the one she got. Colour drained from Fred's face and his skin acquired a clammy sheen as he clutched at the edge of the counter, his knuckles white. He swayed and she thought for a second he might faint.

'She told you. I knew she had. I knew you wouldn't let it go. I saw you out there snooping around at the house.' His voice was strangled and rose several semitones as he spoke. He pulled his shoulders back and came towards her, menacingly slowly, a peculiar expression on his face which had turned almost as red as his hair.

Rose flinched and took a step backwards, unable to scream. 'I don't know what you mean,' she croaked untruthfully, realising what an idiot she had been not to confide in anyone. She saw that he did not believe her. Fear turned to terror. It was so stupid to have come alone, especially when Barry was only a matter of yards away. For God's sake, she thought, come and find me. And then, as Fred swung around and she saw what he was about to do, a voice in her head shouted, Jack, for Christ's sake where are you?

Gwen was serving supper. The radio was on to dispel the gloomy atmosphere of the household. Peter had hardly spoken to her all week. She called him and he came through from the living-room and sat down. She stemmed her irritation at his refusal to discuss what they would do with his inheritance and tried to get the children seated and quiet.

Sensing their father's mood, the children picked up their knives and forks and began to eat.

Gwen sighed. She had had enough. 'Peter, we've got to

talk. We can't go on like this. Oh, now what?' Whoever was at the door could have chosen a more convenient time to call. Gwen went to answer it.

'Yes?' She tossed her head and the short fair hair fell immaculately back into place.

'Gwendoline Pengelly?' She nodded and bit her lip. She did not know the man but she guessed who he was. 'Detective Inspector Pearce. I'd like, to clarify a couple of points. May I come in for a minute?'

'We're just having our meal.'

'I won't keep you long.'

'All right,' she said begrudgingly and flung open the living-room door. She stepped aside and followed him in. The room was gloomy, the light had faded. Gwen impatiently flicked on a table lamp.

'Who is it?' Peter called, getting up from the table.

'It's the police. I've got to answer some more questions. You go and finish your supper or you'll be late for work. You can put mine in the oven. What do you want?' she asked rudely when Peter had returned to the kitchen.

'One of my officers called before, not long after Mrs Pengelly's death. You said at the time that you hadn't seen her for weeks. We now have information that you were seen turning into the drive on the day of your mother-in-law's death and that you were there again afterwards. Perhaps you'd like to clarify this?' Out of the corner of his eye Jack had seen a small movement in the gap of the door. Peter Pengelly was listening outside. So be it, he thought.

Gwen's hand was at her throat, nervously fingering a silver Celtic cross on a chain. She licked her lips. 'I did go there but I couldn't get in. I thought the back door may've been unlocked.'

'And the reason for your visit?'

'I thought I'd clean the place up a bit.'

'So why not ask Martin for a key?'

'I didn't know where to find him.'

Jack took this at face value. If she had intended helping herself to some of Dorothy's bits and pieces she had not succeeded. 'And the first time?'

'It was about tea-time. Peter was at work and the children were next door.'

'And you spoke to Mrs Pengelly?'

'Yes, of course I did. Oh, I see what you mean. She was fine. Really she was.' Gwen bowed her head. 'I wanted to persuade her to give up the house, to go into a home. It's far too big for one old lady, and Peter and I could have done with the money. Anyway, I was worried about her.'

Jack ignored the lie. If her daughter-in-law had been in the least concerned she would have visited far more frequently. 'Did you argue?'

Gwen decided there was nothing for it but to tell the truth. Neither she nor Jack knew that it was Jobber who had seen her and made the call to the station. He had mumbled his name, passed on the information then hung up before he could be questioned further.

'No more than usual. She wasn't an easy woman to get on with.'

'Can you clarify that statement? What were you arguing about?'

'I think I can do that for you.'

'Peter!' Gwen spun around. 'How long have you been listening?'

'Long enough. My wife couldn't stand my mother, Inspector. All she was interested in was getting her hands on her money. You see, Gwen always thought my mother was beneath her. She wouldn't even take the children up there.'

'Oh, Peter, don't, please.' The redness of her face showed her humiliation.

'You see, my mother once told us we would get what we deserved. I think I understand now what she meant. I think I can even guess what she's done.'

Jack said nothing. He knew what the will contained. What interested him was the conversation which had taken place that Thursday tea-time. 'I need to know exactly what was said,' he continued.

Gwen swallowed hard as tears filled her eyes. 'I shouted at her. I called her a selfish old woman. But she was all right when I left her, I swear it.' She turned back to her husband. 'You must believe me, Peter, you must.'

Peter remained rigid and avoided her eyes but Jack believed her. From what he knew of Dorothy it would not have surprised him if she had given the younger woman a run for her money.

'Have you ever taken Nardil, Mrs Pengelly?'

'Nardil? What's that?' Her astonishment was genuine.

'It doesn't matter. That's all for now. I'll see myself out and leave you to get on with your meal.'

He was about to step outside when his bleeper went. 'I'm sorry, may I use your telephone?' Peter waved a hand to indicate where it stood.

'Sir? Where are you? We couldn't get you on the car radio.'

He heard the words 'Fred Meecham', the name of one of Dorothy's friends, but when he heard Barry and Rose's names too he felt sick. Slamming down the handset he was out of the door and into the car in almost one movement. With tyres screeching he drove to the shop.

Barry was studying the other drinkers and found he was enjoying doing so. No wonder Rose took so much pleasure in watching people. Because he was beginning to unwind he did not, at first, notice how long she had been gone. He looked at his watch. Something was wrong. He placed his drink on the bar and left the pub.

Outside he looked left and right and wondered which shop she could possibly have gone to. Surely they were all closed now. The streetlights were on, the pavements and road illuminated, but there was no sign of Rose. His stomach knotted in apprehension. How stupid he had been, he ought to have known that there would be more to their outing than a meal. If only she would confide in him more. And why had he not questioned her sudden need for something from a shop when she had had all day in which to buy things? He wiped his forehead and breathed deeply then began walking swiftly in the direction she had taken.

Ahead he saw a couple, hand in hand. It was no use asking them if they had seen a small, auburn-haired woman because they were oblivious to everything but each other. No lights spilt on to the pavement, each shop he came to was in darkness, the closed sign on the door. Until he came to Fred Meecham's premises. There were lights on there and the door was partially open. Unable to see inside because of the display unit behind the window, Barry pushed open the door. It took several seconds for his eyes to adjust. 'Rose,' he cried. 'Oh, Rosie.' With an enormous effort he swallowed the bile which flooded his throat and went inside. 'It's all right, it'll be all right,' he repeated several times as he stepped around the pools of blood and reached for the phone.

Jack's car skidded to a stop as he parked at an angle against the kerb. If Barry Rowe had made the call he knew with a sickening certainty that Rose was hurt or in danger. He could taste the tuna roll he had eaten hours earlier and the coffee he had drunk too quickly. Rose did not want him, Rose only wished to see him as a friend. That was okay, that was good, that was fine by Jack Pearce, but to live without ever seeing her again? For the first time since his father had died he felt as if he might cry.

He was walking through treacle, everything was in slow motion. Ahead of him was an ambulance, its blue light casting its eerie glow over the buildings on either side of the road as it revolved silently. The paramedics were loading a stretcher into the back of the vehicle, the patient invisible from where he was. His knees sagged.

Barry Rowe emerged from the shop doorway pushing up his glasses in that irritating manner. Then, behind him, deathly white and with bloodstains on the front of her dress but apparently unscathed, came Rose. Jack's fear and anguish instantly turned to fury. He ran towards her.

'You stupid bitch, what the hell do you think you're

playing at?' He towered over her, his anger coming from relief in the way a mother's does when a child runs into the road.

Rose took a deep breath and controlled the trembling which threatened to start at any second. 'Inspector Pearce, I was merely doing your job for you. Excuse me, Barry's going to take me home. You can send someone else over to ask your questions.' With as much dignity as she could manage, Rose took Barry's arm and they walked unsteadily back to where he had left the car, neither caring that she was bloodstained.

Her own anger at Jack's treatment of her had prevented her from passing out. As it drained away she clung more tightly to Barry's arm. He helped her into the car and got the key into the ignition on the third attempt. He was shaken himself and thankful that he had had no more than half a pint of beer. And however small a gesture, driving Rose home was at least something he could do for her. Putting the awful scene to the back of his mind he realised he was pleased at the way in which she had spoken to Jack. He did not allow himself to hope that the relationship was over, that would be too much to ask.

Neither of them spoke until they reached the cottage. Staggering, Rose made it inside. 'Please, go, Barry,' she said. 'I'll be all right.' But before he could answer she had fled upstairs and was violently sick.

At her insistence Barry had left. Rose lay in bed, shivering despite the two hot water bottles she had taken up with her. The fear she had felt when Fred grabbed the knife resurrected itself when she thought how close to death she had been. He had screamed at her, cursing her and Dorothy and saying other things which she did not understand. His bereavement, she thought, had sent him mad.

Jack spoke briefly to the two officers who had arrived at the scene before him. Only after Barry and Rose had gone did he step into the shop. Barry, it seemed, had had the sense after he'd rung the emergency services to switch off the shop lights and turn the sign on the door to closed whilst Rose had remained with Fred, trying to stem the bleeding. The ambulance crew had said they believed he'd survive. Jack would have to wait to find out what had preceded their arrival. As Barry had done, he stepped around the pools of blood. From the floor he picked up the knife which Fred used to slice the joints of meat which he kept in the refrigerated counter if customers wanted them thicker than the slicing machine could provide. At some point someone would have to go and see Barry and Rose but he doubted they would be up to answering questions that day and he knew he could not face her himself so soon.

The first thing Rose did upon waking was to ring Laura. She was still shaking and needed to talk to someone before the police arrived, which she knew they would.

'I'll be right over,' Laura said.

Rose replaced the receiver, knowing that what she had said must have come across as gibberish. She was still standing by the phone when she heard the tap on the kitchen door and Laura was there holding out her arms. 'What on earth have you got yourself into this time, girl?'

As Laura made tea Rose explained all that had happened, from the time Jack had told her it was suicide up to his abysmal treatment of her when he had turned up at the shop. She looked up: a figure had passed the kitchen window and Jack Pearce stood in the doorway. Laura let him in. 'I'm off now, Rose. Trevor's sailing this afternoon.'

'I'm sorry. I forgot.'

'Hey. It doesn't matter. What're friends for.' As she turned slowly, Laura's eyes travelled the length of Jack's body. 'You're a bastard,' she said and closed the door quietly behind her.

'She's right,' Rose added in a voice so low he hardly heard her. 'What do you want?'

'Several things, Rose, but firstly and foremost to apologise. You see, I saw the ambulance, I thought it was you, I thought something had happened to you.' He stood just inside the door with his hands in his pockets. Rose was still pale and her eyes were dull. 'I didn't mean to shout. I was scared, scared I'd lost you completely.'

'If you're here to take a statement you'd better sit down.' She refused to look at him, to be influenced by what she knew she would see in his face.

'I am. I have another officer waiting in the car, I just wanted you to know how I felt first.'

Rose closed her eyes and nodded. The sooner it was over with the better. Jack went outside and signalled for someone to join him. It was a female.

When they were all seated Rose spoke of her visit to Audrey Heath in Plymouth and about how Marigold's disappearance had coincided with the stabbing of a man. She went on to say that Marigold had moved to Cornwall and that, for reasons of her own, Dorothy had wanted her to find the map of Plymouth which she had marked with a cross.

'He did it, you see. Fred Meecham killed that man and Dorothy somehow found out about it. I went to the shop and showed him the map. He thought Dorothy had confided in me – she hadn't, but he wouldn't believe me. He went berserk, I didn't really know what he was shouting but, but She stopped, inhaling deeply. 'He picked up the knife and I thought he was going to kill me.' Rose squeezed her forehead between her thumb and forefinger. She felt exhausted. 'I was trying to get out of the shop when it seemed he'd changed his mind, that it wasn't me he meant to harm any more, it was himself. It was so quick I couldn't stop him. He slashed both wrists. It was horrible. He dropped the knife and staggered around and fell to the floor. I grabbed some tea towels from one of the shelves and wrapped them round his wrists. I should've acted faster but the knife was there beside him and I thought he might pick it up again and go for me. Then Barry was there, he turned off the lights and shut the door to stop any customers coming in. The knife . . . the meat knife – Oh, God, it had ham fat on it and blood. I . . .'

'It's all right, Rose. It's all right.' Jack wondered how much of it was his fault. He had told Fred Meecham that it was Rose who had given him his name.

'Rose, can I use the phone?'

'Yes.'

Jack was away for several minutes and she was unable to hear what he said. 'Is there someone who can stay with you? Barry or Laura?'

'No. I'm all right. I'd prefer to be alone.'

'If you're sure. We've got to go now, Rose.' He reached out as if he was about to touch her but either the presence of the female detective or Rose's change of heart stopped him. His own heart was behaving peculiarly. Wrapped in an oversized robe Rose looked very young and very vulnerable and he was partly to blame for the latter because he had helped to get her into the situation.

Rose watched them leave but then remained at the kitchen table, unable to drag herself upstairs to dress.

CHAPTER THIRTEEN

The morning passed and the shock was beginning to wear off. Gratefully Rose remembered that Stella Jackson's dinner party was that evening. She had accepted the invitation with alacrity, delighted to hear that other artists would be present. She wondered if Nick Pascoe would be one of them but although she had rung him back and arranged to meet him for a drink on Tuesday, he hadn't mentioned the Jacksons. It didn't matter, whether he was there or not it was bound to be an interesting evening: her social life was finally starting to expand.

Rose decided to find out how Fred Meecham was faring but she was not sure if the hospital would give her information as she was neither a relative nor a friend.

As she showered in preparation for the party she began to see how much she had to look forward to although she would also like to know the whole story behind Dorothy's death. At least she had proved to Jack Pearce that she had not taken her own life.

Rose decided to travel to St Ives by the branch line train.

It was too dark to appreciate the view from the rails which ran high up along the coastline and overlooked miles and miles of powdery sand running from Hayle and Carbis Bay to St Ives.

The Jacksons lived above their studio and gallery and immediately she entered their apartments she was back in the sixties. The floors were uncarpeted, the boards sanded and polished. Sofas lined the walls, deep and comfortable and half hidden by handmade cushions and woven blankets. Rose saw immediately that the furnishings were not those of her own youth, items purchased or borrowed because of lack of finances. Stella and Daniel had deliberately created this atmosphere but it had not come cheaply. A table held an array of bottles and glasses and from the kitchen came the unmistakable smell of chilli. In an A-line calf-length denim skirt, a cream frilled shirt and a waistcoat Rose blended in with the other guests as if she had known them all her life.

Stella put an arm across her shoulders and led her around the room, stopping at the table to hand her a drink. 'We're so pleased you could come,' she said, smiling. Her teeth were uneven and one pupil did not move as quickly as the other but beneath her straight black hair, cut just below her ears, her quirky face portrayed a lazy sexuality.

Rose had had time to study the other guests and felt only a slight disappointment that Nick Pascoe was not one of them.

When one of Stone's taxis came to pick her up Rose felt exhilarated. The conversation had ranged from art to politics, from literature to the theatre, and she knew that soon she would host such an evening of her own.

In the morning she sang as the kettle boiled, not very tunefully nor very loudly, but she was out of practice lately. It did not matter that a gale force wind was rattling the windows and bringing down more leaves. To Rose they looked beautiful as they skittered across the grass, their reds and golds colours she would capture in oils.

In the sitting-room she stood in the window, steam from her coffee misting the glass, and watched the waves battering the reinforced wall of the Promenade as they had done since it was built and would continue to do as long as it stood.

So many new and exciting people had entered her life that it was difficult to feel sorry for Fred. But it still hurt to think of Dorothy. There was plenty of time until she was due to collect Martin and take him over to Truro.

'Oh, no.' She backed away from the window but it was too late. Jack had seen her and waved as he strode up the path. She pulled her dressing-gown more tightly around her and went out to the kitchen.

'Don't be angry,' were his words of greeting. 'Knowing your curiosity I thought you'd want to hear the outcome.'

'Come in. Coffee?'

'Please.'

Rose made instant and handed him a mug, omitting to ask him to sit down.

'Meecham's going to pull through – it wasn't as bad as it looked.'

Rose nodded, biting her lip, guessing that Fred would have wished it otherwise. 'I think all he wanted was someone to love him, someone of his own.' She was sure he had begun

246

life as a decent man but circumstances and insecurity had changed him. Looking up she saw what was going through Jack's mind. She ought not to have mentioned love.

'Yes. He lost his first wife, then his son. We now know he paid regular visits to Plymouth to visit prostitutes, one in particular. Marigold Heath. It was the old story. He fell for her in a big way and wanted to take her away from it all, to save her, if you like. The irony is that, in a way, he did, despite the fact that he, a church-going man, was frequenting such a woman.' Jack took a few sips of his coffee. 'You should've told us about the map, Rose, and you were extremely foolish not to mention those threatening calls.'

She remained silent although she had noticed the use of the plural pronoun which depersonalised the conversation. 'What'll happen to him?'

'Psychiatric reports. All that.'

'He won't last, you know.'

'He may not go to prison.'

'I didn't mean that. I don't think he wants to live, not now. He spent all those years with Marigold, firstly protecting her from that pimp of hers, killing him for her sake, then protecting her from gossip. That's why they didn't marry, isn't it? Because he, or they, thought that it would draw attention to themselves and that someone might make the connection. A sister's always a safe bet.'

'You're probably right. He's confessed, Rose, to the murder of Harvey, that's the man in Plymouth and to murdering Dorothy. You understand that this mustn't go any further, there's his trial to come yet and—'

'You don't need to tell me, Jack.'

'No. I'm sorry. It's . . . well, it's the new circumstances, I'm not sure how to deal with you.'

Rose turned away to hide a smile. Deal with her? Was she that awkward?

'Marigold was involved too. She'd told him how Harvey treated her, he was a sadist, and there was no way he was going to let her walk off into the sunset. They set it up together. Heath led Meecham to him. It was as easy as that. Then he provided her with an alibi. Heath made sure she was seen with Harvey earlier in the evening, as she would have expected to have been, and he was fine when she left him. Meecham wasn't known in Plymouth and there was no reason why he should have come under suspicion. He'd booked a hotel room, a double, and made a show of taking her up mere but they slipped out later. When he got back to Cornwall the next day he put it around that his sister was coming to live with him.'

'Dorothy knew all this, is that why he killed her?'

'Yes, Dorothy knew, or guessed. She'd been unpacking some china with a view to selling it. It was wrapped in old newspaper. She happened to come across a report and put two and two together.'

Rose frowned. It was unlike Dorothy not to have done anything. Then she remembered that the unpacking would have been recent and she had done something, she had put the map in an envelope for Rose to find, trusting her not to do anything until Marigold had been buried. Maybe Dorothy suspected how Fred would react if he was confronted, maybe she was trusting him, too, to do the right thing.

'But why was Dorothy selling her things?'

'This is strictly between you and me. She was setting up a trust fund for Martin. She wanted Hinkston to provide prints or replicas of everything she sold him in case Peter and Gwen noticed the missing items and made life difficult. She was terrified they'd get a doctor in to say she was unfit to live on her own. We know that the daughter-in-law went up there and an argument took place, but I suspect Gwen Pengelly got her money's worth from your friend.'

'I'd like to think so.'

'Anyway, Meecham went up there as well, a couple of nights before her death. It was late in the evening. He was intending to make one last attempt at squeezing money out of Dorothy and to soften her up had taken along a bottle of decent whisky. He knew it wasn't something she normally drank and he imagined, quite correctly, that a few glasses would do the trick. But again she refused his request, as he'd expected she would, but then she made the fatal mistake of telling him what she knew, what she had read in that old report in the *Western Morning News*. He denied it and left, forgetting to take the whisky with him. He knew he had to act quickly or Dorothy might go to the police. We now know that whilst he was in Truro and had begun seeing Marigold he'd suffered from severe depression, caused by guilt, the psychiatrist believes, because he was frequenting prostitutes, and also because he knew he was going to kill Harvey, that at some point he would have to. Meanwhile he moved to Hayle and life started to improve so he didn't get around to taking the Nardil that was prescribed for him. Like Dorothy, Meecham didn't sign on with a doctor here, that's why we couldn't trace where the drug came from.'

'Poor Dorothy, first Gwen has a go at her, then Fred kills her. But how did he do it?'

'Ground up the pills to powder and went out there on the pretence that he wanted to apologise. He said they might as well have some of the whisky. It affected Dorothy very quickly and he topped up her glass, adding more of the Nardil. He watched her die.'

'Oh, Jack!'

'On his previous visit he had called her a hypocrite, saying she didn't spend any money and she begrudged it to a dying woman. That's when Dorothy had explained that he was the bigger hypocrite with his church-going ways when she knew what he had done. She was probably already exhausted on that final visit after having dealt with Gwen earlier.'

'Thank you for telling me.'

'That's okay.'

She stood. 'I have to get ready to go out. Goodbye, Jack,' she said quietly but with a certain finality.

Jack didn't reply. He turned to leave, knowing that what he had had with Rose would never be again.

The wind howled, rocking the car. Through the windscreen his vision was blurred for several seconds but it wasn't raining. He sighed. Yes, they would meet from time to time but Rose Trevelyan had become a different person.

At eleven she picked Martin up at the gate of Jobber's farm. He was dressed in his best, his hair slicked down with water. Making general conversation they drove into the city and parked the car. Martin was still pale and his hands shook but the blankness had gone from his eyes. Being with Jobber was the best thing that could have happened to him.

Together they entered the old building which was smartly decorated inside, and were asked to take a seat. Peter and Gwen arrived seconds after them. The words of their greetings were cordial but Rose sensed an underlying hostility on Gwen's part. She had promised to stay and give Martin a lift back as the solicitor had said he would not detain them long.

'Ah, good morning.' Henry Peachy was tall and thin with deep lines etched in his face. He wore a suit which was by no means new and his shoulders were stooped but what struck Rose was his warm smile and something about his eyes which suggested that he was content with his lot and that there was little which could disturb his equanimity. Shaking hands with them individually he glanced inquisitively at Rose.

'I gave Martin a lift,' she explained. 'I'm Mrs Trevelyan, I was a friend of Dorothy's. Can I wait here or shall I come back later?'

'Mrs Rose Trevelyan?'

'Yes.'

'In that case, my dear, you might as well join us. This involves you too.'

Rose felt Gwen's eyes on the back of her head and was glad she could not see the expression in them. They followed Mr Peachy to a room at the end of the corridor. It was not an office, it housed only a large walnut table and eight chairs.

'I thought we'd be more comfortable here.' Henry Peachy placed some papers on the table and invited them to sit down. 'I knew Mrs Pengelly for many years,' he began. 'I suppose you could say that she was more than a client. I can't tell you how sorry I was not to be able to attend her funeral.

'Now, before we get down to business I've asked for some coffee to be sent in.'

There was a strained silence while they waited for it although the solicitor seemed not to notice as he continued to study what was in front of him. When it arrived he indicated that they should all help themselves.

'I think it'll be easier if I read out Mrs Pengelly's instructions first, then if there are any queries I'll be happy to answer them for you.' Methodically he went through the heading of the will. Then, "To Peter James Pengelly I leave the property known as Venn's Farm."'

Rose's head was tilted slightly as she tried to gauge Gwen's reactions without appearing to. She seemed to be smirking but hid it by raising a hand to her mouth then pushing back her fair hair. Rose, having been through something similar, began to see that Gwen had misunderstood the statement.

'"To Joseph Robert Hicks I leave one thousand pounds and the Queen Victoria Jubilee mug of which he is so fond. To my friend, Rose Trevelyan, I leave one thousand pounds and a Beryl Cook original of her choice of three."'

But Rose wasn't listening. She was delighted at Jobber's bequest although it had taken her a couple of seconds to realise who Joseph Robert was. But there had been no mention of Martin. Had Jack been wrong? Something registered. She looked up, her mouth open. Henry Peachy was smiling at her, he repeated what he had just read out.

'*And* a Beryl Cook? Oh, how wonderful.' She grinned around the room. Only Martin grinned back. He seemed unconcerned or unaware of the way things were going.

Mr Peachy coughed and continued. '"The residue of my estate I leave to Martin John Pengelly."'

Another silence followed until Gwen had worked out what this meant. 'No, that can't be right.'

'It is perfectly correct, Mrs Pengelly. Your mother-in-law's wishes are quite clearly stated. You may see for yourself if you choose.'

'But what's he going to do with it all?'

'That is for Mr Pengelly to decide. Of course, none of this takes place with immediate effect. Probate has to be proved. Now, is there anything you'd like to ask me?'

Rose and Martin shook their heads, Peter stared down at his hands. 'Mother's done the right thing,' he said.

Gwen jerked around in her chair. 'Don't be ridiculous. Can't we challenge this? She can't have been in her right mind when she made this will. What about us? We've got the children to think of.'

Henry Peachy hid his indignation well. 'My client was of perfectly sound mind when she came to me with her instructions and we have discussed the matter again recently regarding a trust fund when she provided me with a list of all her valuables and their estimated worth. We also have a record of her savings. As executors my firm has been instructed to arrange for the sale of any goods Mrs Pengelly has not been able to dispose of, the proceeds of which are to be placed in the said trust fund for Martin.'

There seemed to be nothing more to say. Gwen and Peter left first, followed by Martin and then Rose who had stopped to thank Mr Peachy. At the door she took Martin's arm. 'Great, isn't it? You'll never have to worry now.' But Martin was too bemused to reply.

Back at the farm she went in with him to tell Jobber the good news. Tears filled his eyes. 'I always had my tea in that mug, she never cared that it was worth a bit. Still, the boy's taken care of, that's what matters.' They had a celebratory drink then Rose drove home planning where to hang the painting and what sort of car she would exchange the Mini for.

Peter and Gwen did not speak on the drive back to Hayle. When they reached the house Peter remained in the car. 'I'm going for a drive. Alone,' he said. At some point since his mother's death he had come to see how much Gwen had influenced him where Dorothy was concerned. 'You're sick, do you know that? Martin deserves it, he deserves the whole bloody lot if you ask me.'

'I'm sorry, Peter. Look, at least we'll be able to move.'

'Will we?' He crunched the gears, prior to pulling away from the kerb. 'You're forgetting that the house was left to me. It's my decision whether we stay here or move to Venn's Farm. When I've made up my mind you can decide what you're going to do.'

With a sinking feeling Gwen watched him drive away. She knew what his decision would be and that she would have to spend the rest of her life in that awful place without enough money to restore it for years.

Rose stopped at the Co-op in Newlyn and bought a bottle of champagne. It was far too early in the day to be drinking but she didn't care. Once home, she placed it in the freezer section of the fridge to chill quickly. A new car and the painting, a new life and a date with Nick Pascoe tomorrow – and the mystery of Dorothy's death had been solved. So had another, one which had taken place years ago, Harvey's, and she, Rose, had helped to solve it. 'I deserve it,' she said as she popped the cork and watched the pale gold liquid effervesce in her glass.

On Monday night Nick Pascoe lay in bed, his hands clasped behind his head. He was smiling. Tomorrow he was seeing Rose Trevelyan. He did not know which excited him more, the woman herself or her painting.